D0340393

Lock & Mori

LOCK & MORI

HEATHER W. PETTY

SIMON & SCHUSTER BFYR

New York   London   Toronto   Sydney   New Delhi

An imprint of Simon & Schuster Children's Publishing Division
1230 Avenue of the Americas, New York, New York 10020
SIMON & SCHUSTER BFYR is a trademark of Simon & Schuster, Inc.
For information about special discounts for bulk purchases, please contact Simon & Schuster Special Sales at 1-866-506-1949 or business@simonandschuster.com.
The Simon & Schuster Speakers Bureau can bring authors to your live event. For more information or to book an event, contact the Simon & Schuster Speakers Bureau at 1-866-248-3049 or visit our website at www.simonspeakers.com.
Book design by Krista Vossen
The text for this book is set in Bembo.
Manufactured in the United States of America
10 9 8 7 6 5 4 3 2 1
Library of Congress Cataloging-in-Publication Data
Petty, Heather.
Lock & Mori / Heather Petty. — First edition.
pages cm
Summary: In modern-day London, sixteen-year-old Miss James "Mori" Moriarty is looking for an escape from her recent past and spiraling home life when she takes classmate Sherlock Holmes up on his challenge to solve a murder mystery.
ISBN 978-1-4814-2303-8 (hardcover : alk. paper) — ISBN 978-1-4814-2305-2 (eBook)
[1. Mystery and detective stories. 2. Characters in literature—Fiction. 3. Love—Fiction.
4. Family problems—Fiction. 5. London (England)—Fiction. 6. England—Fiction.] I. Title.
II. Title: Lock and Mori.
PZ7.1.P48Lo 2015
[Fic]—dc23
2014028105

To my mother,
who will never read this
but lives on every page

London, Present Day

I wore a hat with a feather plume the first time I met Sherlock Holmes. It was the fourth of March. I only remember the date because all three of my brothers glommed onto the Marching Forth pun for the entirety of breakfast. Freddie even had a stupid, hollering ringtone for his mobile that shouted, "March FOOOORTH!" over and over until I threatened to flush the thing down the toilet. For once, leaving for school felt more like bliss than drudgery. But the bliss didn't linger.

First was double maths, where yet again I was forced to explain that just because our professor was ignorant of the latest in math theory, it didn't mean he could mark my home-work wrong when clearly it was the book that was in error. Next came economics and a lecture from books I'd read for fun last summer's break. Lunch was followed by a long, boring lab as Marcus Gregson turned our chemistry experiment into a black, smoldering thing that stank up the entire room. How he managed to do so, despite the two contingencies I'd put in place to make it impossible for him to ruin it, the greatest detective in history would never be able to deduce. I warned

Marcus his calculations were off, but Professor made me promise to let him run at least one lab on his own before term was over. Not my fault her room would smell like chemical warfare for months.

I thought I'd escaped the madness when I settled into my final class of the day, but even that turned into a colossal cock-up. Still, I hadn't quite expected that a fire drill would send me into the inner sanctum of the most eccentric, highly notorious boy in my class. And by the time that happened, it had already been a very, very long day, to say the least—the kind of day that could only ever end with me wearing a feathered hat.

The very minute the fire alarm started to simultaneously scream and flash lights at us, Miss Francis, the drama teacher, instructed the class to calmly make their way out of the theater, except for me. She said, "Mori, do be an angel and nip downstairs to storage to fetch our Mr. Holmes."

Miss Francis was always calling us angels and champs. "Can he not hear the alarm on his own?" I asked.

She might have nodded or shook her head, but she was already pushing me out the theater's side door, so I couldn't see. "Sherlock doesn't seem to pay attention to things like alarms when he's working. Be quick about it, will you?"

I, of course, had heard of Sherlock Holmes and his secret lab in the basement of the theater. It was just cartoonish enough of an image to spread widely around the school. He found the chemistry lab inadequate to his needs, which was the only part of the story that had intrigued me, and his mother had somehow talked the headmaster into letting him have a space of his own. I suspected she used Headmaster's favorite kind of persuasion—the monetary kind.

I spent my trip down the steps to the shadowy basement hall picturing what a lab that so outshined our chem lab would be like and wincing against the flashing fire-drill lights, which were all the brighter in the dim. It wasn't until I swept open the double doors of the storage room he used as a workshop that I remembered I was still in full costume, from hat to lacy trim, which barely brushed the dusty linoleum floors of the hall. I wasn't too embarrassed, however, because Sherlock's hair stood up on one side, almost as tall as my plume. With his back to me, he ran fingers through his mop, readily displaying how it had gotten that way.

The lab itself was fairly unimpressive—two long tables with all the basics: glassware, tubes, flames, and even a centrifuge and an autoclave. But instead of brown glass bottles full of chemicals for experiments, Sherlock's shelves were stacked with specimen containers, Baggies filled with various samples, and books—stacks and stacks of books on every subject imaginable, from *Who's Who* to physics, mountaineering to criminology. I probably would have continued to explore were it not for the constant screeching reminder of why I was there.

"What is it?" Sherlock shouted over the alarm, without turning to acknowledge me. Instead, he hunched farther over the table in front of him, one hand typing furiously at a tablet, while his other carefully turned a small plastic knob to adjust the flow of red fluid from what looked like an ancient glass

IV bottle. The red substance dripped down a tube and into a cup with a rather alarming rhythm.

"I'm to fetch you," I shouted back. My voice barely carried over the blaring fire alarm.

"I cannot hear you, so you might as well go away." His arms flew into the air as he spoke, then dived down again, adjusting vials, tubes, and the flames of several Bunsen burners. He moved around the table with an odd sort of violent grace, like a mad symphony conductor directing the bubbles and billows, until finally he was facing me, though he did not look up. His school uniform was as disheveled as his lab: white shirt wrinkled and untucked, with sleeves rolled up to his elbows; navy-and-silver-striped tie loosened and askew; and blue sweater flung over the side of a chair so that one sleeve pooled on the dusty floor.

"I'm to fetch you," I shouted again, adding, "because of the alarm," which immediately silenced.

He did look up then, his dark blue eyes fiery with what appeared to be a form of righteous indignation, though his expression dulled to pure intrigue as he took in my appearance.

"You must come out to the courtyard when the alarm—"

"Edwardian?" He focused in on the buttons of my bodice, and it was all I could do to keep my hands from adjusting the neckline rather higher.

"Late Victorian," I corrected. "But you—"

"Just a moment." Sherlock scowled as he reached to flip his tablet back around to face him. He squinted at the screen and mumbled, "Period costuming," as he typed one-handed.

"What about it?"

He followed my gaze down to his screen. "Topics I have not yet mastered."

"You wish to master period costuming?" My hand slid up to rest on my hip as my lips formed the smile that most infuriated my father. It appeared to have no such effect on Sherlock.

"Asks the girl dressed to meet Her Highness Victoria."

"Point," I conceded.

"Ah, we're keeping score. Good to know."

I rolled my eyes, and then a silence fell between us that normally would have been my cue to dash, but the way he was staring made me feel squirmy. "I came from the theater, just now." I waved my copy of the play in the space between us by way of explanation, though I wasn't sure why I felt the need to explain myself to him. "It's a graded performance of—"

"An Oscar Wilde. I'm not sure our school's theater performs anyone else."

I started to affirm that it was indeed an Oscar Wilde, but apparently the boy wasn't finished with his guessing.

"You're the understudy, though you'd rather not be. You took this class for some reason other than your love of the art form." I opened my mouth to speak, but he stepped closer, his finger in the air. "Possible that it's a family craft, and you do it to please a parent. Father? No, mother."

I held back a sigh and stared at him until I was very sure he was done. He had already interrupted me three times in our short conversation, and I wasn't sure I could repress my violent tendencies were he to cut me off once more.

"Close, but no." Truth? He was almost exactly right. But I wasn't about to feed the enormous monster of an ego that he displayed with every condescending quirk of his thin, girlish eyebrows. He would score no more points off me.

"Nonsense. That dress is at least two sizes too small, and not at all fitted for your figure, which is"—a soft pink skirted his cheek as he stared at my corset again—"endowed." Only his deepening blush saved him from my outrage. "And despite my admitted lack of mastery on the subject, I do not for a moment believe that orange trainers were popular in late Victorian times. Then there's the matter of your worn and tattered copy of the play, which, by the dated doodles I can now see on the cover, definitely belonged to your mother."

"Are you quite done?" I asked, much more gently than I felt. I might also have slid my hands over the doodles in question. My mother had gone through some kind of Duran Duran obsession, apparently.

"Are you ready to admit that my observations are correct?"

"There are more pressing concerns." I glanced behind him, but he didn't take the cue.

"Nothing is more pressing than the truth."

I gave him one last chance to follow my gaze back to his table, and when he did not, I sighed. "Fine. I am always the understudy, as I learn lines rather more quickly than is typical. I also have no interest in any of the graded tracks in class, and being on call for the actors gets me out of having to paint sets, run lights, or direct. In all, it is easy and makes me look well rounded to university gatekeepers. That, and that alone, is why I take drama." I nodded to sell the lie but betrayed myself by clutching the script more tightly in my hands. He stared into my eyes, but I didn't for a moment think he'd missed my gaffe. "The trainers are what I brought to wear home from school today. As you noted, the ailing actress whose place I'm taking in the rehearsal is smaller than me, and while I can stuff myself into her costume, I could not make my feet shrink three sizes to wear her slippers. Now, as to the more pressing matter—"

"Eidetic?" Sherlock asked, adding, "Your memory. It is what allows you to learn the lines."

If I hadn't thought it would entertain him utterly, I might have growled aloud before I answered with a curt, "Yes."

I shouldn't have said. He stepped toward me, some of the fire returning to his gaze—as though I were a flask of liquid that had suddenly turned an intriguing shade of scarlet. But then he narrowed his eyes, studying my face as he spoke again. "I'm not wrong about your mother. That copy of the play was hers."

I narrowed my eyes in mocking return, but the way he spoke of my mother so freely set me on edge.

"My mother is—is dead." I hadn't meant to say that, exactly. But I was determined not to show him my internal surprise. Nor was I ready to hear his theories on why I kept taking drama in homage to her memory. So I leaned enticingly close to Sherlock Holmes, so close that I noticed how the blue of his eyes was the exact same shade as my own. And then I whispered, "I believe that you should go back to your tubes and burners now."

He took in a deep breath, and I felt a trace of his exhale against my cheek as he asked, "And why is that?"

I leaned back enough to stand up straight and offered him my best smile. "Your blood is overflowing." I spun round to leave just after I'd spoken, though I took enormous pleasure in the fading sounds of his scrambling and cursing as I walked away.

Chapter 2

Albert Einstein once said, "The monotony of a quiet life stimulates the creative mind."

Gandhi said, "Monotony is the law of nature," like the rising of the sun day after day.

I tend to side with the ladies on this subject, like Edith Wharton, who called it "the mother of all the deadly sins," or Anaïs Nin, who, in her simple way, said, "Monotony, boredom, death."

It's why I carried dice in my pocket, one black and two whites. Running probabilities was an easy way to calm my thoughts, and the fall of the dice was unpredictable but straightforward, while still providing an uncomplicated backdrop for my thinking. I'm not some übergenius who feels compelled to chant equations while tromping the halls, but maths come rather easier to me than to most. I follow the path of an equation like a string through a maze. And I enjoy the puzzle of it.

Some days, like that March 4, when the idea of taking the same bus home to the same stop to the same sidewalk made me want to shriek loudly and in public, I used my dice to break the monotony. The dice gave me an excuse to try something new. And after my ridiculously irritating day, a little newness appealed.

After a late rehearsal I changed out of the gown and into jeans and a sweater, instead of my uniform. I hated wearing my uniform home; it drew the worst kind of attention. It made me approachable. Once my costume was put away, I pulled out the dice and rolled them across the dressing room counter, with a result of Black = 1, White = 1, White = 1. One chance in 216 to get a roll like that. The strangeness of it might have been an omen, if I believed that the hidden powers of the universe applied omens to dice games. Or if I believed in omens at all.

In my game, the black die told me what transport I'd take, bus for odd and tube for even, and the whites told me which bus and stop to take. Any cockeyed dice meant I'd be walking the whole way. I had to completely plan the trip in my mind before taking my first step. It was my way of memorizing my part of London. My roll meant I'd take the first bus and get off at the first stop.

Unfortunately, the first bus that came was the 27, which was the bus I would've taken without the game, because the first stop was less than a block and a half from home. It was literally the shortest possible commute to come from the longest of odds. So, I decided to go with the spirit of the dice rather than be ruled by them, and walked down to Gloucester Place, then didn't cross over to Baker until Crawford. It was technically going the wrong way first, but it turned a two-minute walk into a ten-minute walk, the longest way round the block.

Near the corner of Baker Street and Crawford, the odds really took over. Sadie Mae Jackson walked out of Boots pharmacy just as I was walking past. If one of us had been looking down or even out at traffic, we might have pretended not to see each other, passed without acknowledgment, and carried on with our lives, as we did whenever school forced our proximity. But that day our eyes met directly when we were mere feet apart.

I was taken once again by their disarming shade of amber—the very thing that had made me stare at her that first day we'd met. Maths, of course. As was typical, I was done with our class work when we still had a half hour of class left, and with nothing to do, I glanced around, tried to see if I could guess when the rest of the students in class would be done as well. I'd only noticed her eye color when she'd given the equations scrawled out on the side chalkboard a strangled look. I grinned at her expression, and she caught me staring.

"Or you could just keep sitting there like a possum playin' dead," she'd said, as if we were in the middle of a conversation, not the beginning.

I was pretty sure I hadn't missed her saying anything else. Her eyes weren't that disarming. "Or what?"

"I thought you were fixin' to help me with this impossible graphing nonsense, but if you'd rather stick with the possum eyes . . ."

That's when she'd bugged out her amber eyes, evidently

like a possum, and I'd narrowed mine. I helped her, though, even when it meant meeting after class to explain all the math theory behind the problem dating back to the beginning of the school year. She'd offered to help me with literature, and I let her, despite the fact that I'd done all the reading months prior. She was keen on paying back a favor—not that I ever felt that Sadie owed me anything.

She definitely didn't owe me anything outside of Boots on this day. And she almost immediately looked past me, which for a moment made me think we were going back to pretending, but then her body moved toward me, like I was pulling a lifeline secured around her middle. When she moved close enough for me to recognize the smattering of darker brown freckles that didn't quite blend into the brown of her skin, I noticed she was still wearing the locket her grandmother had given her before she left America. Her hair was longer now, the soft spirals falling around her ears rather than spiking out from her scalp in what had been her signature look all last year.

We stood awkwardly for a few fidgety seconds that felt like eternities before she spoke. "Somebody ought to say something, I s'pose. Might as well be me."

Say something, I echoed bitterly in my mind. As if saying something now would erase the six months of nothing we'd had. Sadie had been the closest to a best friend I'd ever known. She'd come to England for what was supposed to be just a single school year. She'd stayed on, though, to try for A-levels and a spot at university. At least, that had been her plan before. I had no idea what she was planning now.

I tried very hard to shrug and walk away, but her too-familiar American drawl tugged something loose in my mind until all my favorite memories of her filled all the empty gaps between my thoughts like sand pouring through stones in a jar, shifting away the time we'd spent apart like it was nothing. I grinned, despite the ache of that.

My smile was seemingly all the encouragement she needed. She said, "I shouldn't have stopped calling, and I know that, I do." She twisted her shopping bag until the canvas handles creaked, then watched as it spun loose. "I told myself I was giving you time and space, but then the not calling came easier than the calling. Truth is, I didn't know what to say."

There was nothing to say—that's what I wanted to tell her right then, but the aching got worse with the thought of the nights I'd spent wishing the phone would ring to help me escape. And by the time the words tumbled out, I said, "You don't have to say this."

"Now, Mori, I'm trying very hard to apologize, as my nana would have me do. You don't want me to get in trouble with my nana, do you?"

I attempted a flat grin. "I assume she's still in America."

"Yes, indeed. And while you've never been subject to her Talking-To, I will tell you it has a longer reach than the Atlantic Ocean." Sadie smiled. "I've missed you something awful."

I nodded, because I'd missed her too, but I couldn't seem to say it aloud. Perhaps it was harder to make up with someone when you haven't fought, really. Just drifted. Even though it appeared we were going to take one step back toward each other in front of Boots, one step doesn't cross a six-month chasm all at once. Especially not the six months I'd had.

I was silent too long, and Sadie Mae started up again, like she always did. She couldn't stand quiet between us. There was something comforting about her prattling on, though. Perhaps we'd taken more than one step after all.

"I won't keep you, 'cause I know you have your studies. But I'll look for you at school tomorrow, if that's okay. I do hope that's okay?"

I nodded. "I'd like that."

She rested her hand on my arm and leaned close. "We'll work our way up to the calling."

Sadie left with a wink and a more genuine smile than I'd seen on her in months of accidental sightings. I wasn't ready to go home, though, so I retraced my steps around the block and gave myself ten more minutes of thinking time.

Ten minutes wasted as it turned out. By the time I marked the corner to Baker Street, my thoughts were lost in reliving my encounters with both Sadie Mae and the great enigma, Sherlock Holmes. I'd heard so many rumors about the boy, I half thought he might be hunchbacked with the crazed white hair and chemical-stained fingers of a mad scientist. He could have at least worn a lab coat over his school uniform—live up to the stereotype.

I was, in fact, so caught up in the memory of our meeting, I didn't notice the music coming out of my house until it was too late. I couldn't have done anything about it were I pay-ing attention. Run. I perhaps could've run off, waited it out somewhere else. Not for the first time, I thought how pathetic it was to be afraid of your own house. Especially since my home used to feel like the safest place in the city.

We had our very own police detail, or so my mom would joke whenever Dad paced the halls of our tiny house, making sure every door was bolted, every window locked.

"Promise I won't try to escape, constable," she'd say, holding her hands in the air and quirking the selfsame smile I must have inherited from her. Constable Moriarty, Detective Constable Moriarty, Detective Sergeant Moriarty—my dad was on his way to becoming Detective Inspector of the Metropolitan Police Service, Westminster Borough. And then Mum got sick. I couldn't remember the last time Dad secured our house. Maybe he no longer cared if anyone entered. Or escaped.

I counted three open windows as I walked up the steps to our door, each allowing the warbling piano to tumble down toward me just before the trumpet took its turn to bleat out the simple melody of "Memories of You" by Louis Armstrong. It was an ancient song, but my parents met volunteering at a city tea dance. Dad said he first laid eyes on Mum as she was fox-trotting around the floor of an old community center in the arms of some pensioner who had better dance skills than my dad. He watched her for five dances before he got up the nerve to ask her for a waltz, and that's when the song came on the stereo. That's when they fell in love.

I thought that kind of love lasted forever. Turns out, it's more fragile than glass.

Louis was singing about a "rosary of tears" by the time I got the courage to open the front door. The calm domestic scene in our kitchen was a bit of an anticlimax, though I saw clues of the coming chaos—a half-empty bottle of bourbon, three glasses filled to different heights with the amber liquid and scattered around the counters and table, which meant that he was already drunk enough to lose track of his tumbler. Dinner was ready, untouched and cooling on the stove, meaning Dad hadn't eaten anything before pouring the stuff down his throat. Wouldn't be long before something set him off.

He emptied the glass in front of him and went back to scrolling for crime news on his laptop, while my nine-year-old brother, Sean, toiled away at his spelling work on the other side of the table. My other brothers, Freddie and Michael, knew better than to come out of hiding on "Memories of You" nights—the advantage of being twelve and ten years old rather than Seanie's age. I hoped it wouldn't take another year for Sean to learn.

I squeezed past Seanie's chair to the stove in the silent space between the end of the song and the warbling piano that started it up again. It sounded all the more eerie in its travel from my dad's bedroom and across the hall to where we were.

"Body in the park," Dad grunted. When neither Sean nor I responded, he slammed his fist down on the table and then stared out the window longingly. "Found him 'bout an hour ago. Killed last night."

"Figures, and on your day off, right, Dad?" Sean was somehow convinced that crimes only ever happened when our father wasn't on duty.

"Stay out of the park till the police have it all sorted, yeah?"

Sean smiled, and my heart sank. "They'll never sort it without you, Dad. The police are worthless!"

Everything fell silent as the space between the song's repeats came up again, and I cursed under my breath.

"What did you say, boy?" Dad stood so quickly, he sent his chair flying back to clatter against the counter.

Sean shrank down as Dad advanced on him, his panicked eyes shifting from Dad to me and back. I knew what he'd been trying to do. On any other night, Dad would've cheeked back about the "sodding police" and how pathetic they were without him there. But not when "Memories of You" played. Never then.

"He didn't mean it," I said, but I couldn't distract him from Sean. I couldn't stop him either. Not yet. If I played my cards too soon, it would get so much worse. But it was painful to stand at the counter and do nothing.

"You calling what I do worthless? You couldn't wipe your arse without help."

I watched him tower over Sean, as solid as a statue, watched his hand rise in the air. I flinched before I heard the smacking thud of Dad's fist against Sean's jaw but didn't look away, not even when a stream of apologies bubbled from Sean's lips in that simpering tone that only ever fed Dad's anger.

Before his fist could fall again, I was there, standing tall between them, infuriating smile sliding easily onto my lips.

17

I tried to find Dad's eyes in the sunken shadows of his face. I tried to show him I wasn't even a little afraid, but inside I was cringing. Waiting. Preparing. He wouldn't hit me—or, at least, he hadn't yet. But not all strikes are done with a fist.

"Out of my way, cow."

"You never called Mum that," I quipped back, earning the full glare of his wrath. "Cow" was probably the kindest thing he'd call me when he was drunk. He always got worse and louder, stood closer so that I had to smell him and feel his spit on my cheek. If there were any other way to make him leave us alone, I would've done it.

"You think you're like her? You think you can take her place? Think you can wear her nobility like one of your whore outfits?"

I didn't respond, just stood still, trying to block his view of Sean.

"You're nothing like her, you filthy slag. She was an angel. You're nothing."

I watched his gaze drift again toward Sean, who sat frozen in his chair, not whimpering softly enough.

I sighed. When it was just the alcohol, he'd go through a few of his favorite diatribes and then storm off to finish his bottle, usually without hitting anyone. He was always especially creative on "Memories of You" nights—like freeing his fists freed an arsenal of insults, too.

Evidently, I hadn't yet taken enough. I slid my hands up to rest on my hips and attempted to widen my infuriating grin before the next assault on my character began. But as

Dad called me a liar, a street bitch, and every other synonym of whore he had ever learned, unworthy to tread the same floorboards my mother's sacred feet had walked, my mind drifted to the last time I'd struck this very pose. Miraculously, my thoughts filled with tubes and flasks, with the long, thin fingers that adjusted flames to a lower setting, conducting his orchestra of drips and bubbles.

I thought of Sherlock Holmes and his ridiculous mop of hair sticking up in front, and I almost laughed. In fact, before I knew it, Dad was grabbing his bottle, mumbling something about how I wasn't worth his breath and he couldn't stand the sight of me. And finally he stumbled across the hall and into his room.

As soon as the door slammed, Freddie and Michael appeared from the shadows of the staircase and descended on the food. Fred met my eyes guiltily, and I shook my head as I wiped my shirtsleeve across my cheek. Dad turned the music up higher to mask his sobs, but it didn't work. This was the routine on "Memories of You" nights. And, fitting with that routine, I went to the freezer to grab a sack of peas for Sean's face.

"Make a plate for Seanie," I said quietly as my youngest brother snatched the sack from my hand.

"I'm no baby," he snapped. "I'll get my own food."

I resisted the urge to ruffle his hair as I walked by him toward the door to grab my coat.

"Where're you going, Mori?" Michael asked timidly. He glanced out into the darkness of the hall around Dad's door, then back at me. But we both knew he wouldn't come out again—not after one of his crying jags. I'm sure he didn't want us to see him like that. Like hearing wasn't enough for us to realize how pathetic he'd become.

I caught myself staring past Michael and met his eyes with a reassuring smile. "Out."

Chapter 3

The only true benefit of living on Baker Street was its prox-imity to Regent's Park, which provided acres and acres of escape. Unfortunately, even the short walk from our house to the Outer Circle was too long to keep my father's words from catching up to me. I tried to once more focus on the ridiculous boy playing alchemist in the basement of a school theater, but it wasn't enough to block out the echo of the hate in my dad's voice, the feel of the spittle that flew from his lips to my cheek. The disgust in his eyes.

I was thankful for the darkness as I crossed York Bridge into the park proper. I turned left and made sure to keep my head down and only wipe at my eyes when I was in the shadows between path lights. Nothing worse than a complete stranger asking what's wrong and having to come up with some stupid lie about how the dog's run off or a beloved goldfish died. Once my feet were on the grass, the tears flowed more freely.

I wasn't the only one there. I scanned the lawn down to the lake. There had been a murder in the park, according to Dad, but all the regulars were still about. The old woman who looked like a globular thing because of all the bags she had strapped to her body. The man who had a wallet in each of his back pockets and always managed to drop one when he leaned into the rubbish cans to pick out his recyclables. I walked past them and a few silhouettes of people who didn't matter and didn't look up. Some kind of privacy bubble surrounds us whenever we leave civilized things like paths and lamps behind.

The bandstand was deserted, save for one shadowed figure, who almost always seemed to be leaning on the far side of the monument when I came to the park at night. I might not have noticed him at all except for the orange glow that backlit the silhouette of his head when he took a drag from his cigarette. I should've been afraid of him. I used to be afraid to be in the park at night, but that never stopped me from running to it. I was, perhaps, less bothered by a racing heart than a broken one.

I climbed up onto the platform and walked across to the side that faced the lake. The scent of burning cloves surrounded me as I tried my best to convince myself that nothing my dad said meant anything.

Problem was, he wasn't wrong. Not about Mum. She wasn't the pristine saint of our memories, but she was a good mom. Dad didn't drink when she was well. Seanie didn't get hit when she was alive. None of the boys did. And that was on me, because it was my job to take care of them now that she was gone. Even on nights like tonight, when I just wanted to get on a train and never look back. I only didn't because I knew that bedtime would come soon enough, and I'd have to be back at the house to make sure Seanie brushed his teeth.

I sat up straighter and dried my cheeks with the sleeves of my coat one final time, then kicked my feet over the side of the bandstand platform to dangle freely. I could barely make out glimpses of the reflected moon through the long droopy tendrils of the giant willow tree that stood at the shore. The tree looked a little like I felt—weary and alone.

"You didn't tell me your name."

I jolted when the shadowed figure spoke, then again when I realized who was speaking. Hearing Sherlock's voice out in the middle of Regent's Park was so surreal, it took me a moment to realize I wasn't just imagining it.

"Are you talking to me?"

He stepped into the moonlight and I almost didn't recognize him out of his uniform. He was like a different person in his gray peacoat and blue-striped scarf, as put together as he had been rumpled earlier in the day. He pulled a drag from his dark brown cigarette, just as a pack of wiggling dogs jostled past the bandstand, their owner struggling to keep hold of the leashes.

"I don't understand pets," he said, loud enough for the poor grasping woman to hear. "People claim to love their animals but then hoard them in tiny little boxed yards or houses. They force them to act against nature in line with human conveniences. It's a bitter way to show love, yes?"

He didn't wait for me to answer, instead blew out some smoke and kept on with his tirade. "If one truly loved animals, wouldn't she rather see them live wild and free? Not domesticated and caged and humiliated, as servants to be ordered about."

When the owner walked out of earshot, Sherlock took another quick drag and blew it out after her, then turned back to me.

"Sorry. I didn't mean to interrupt your private moment, but I realized after you left my lab that I never asked your name." When I didn't answer, Sherlock slid one hand in his pocket and with the other flicked ash into the breeze. "I've seen you here many times and never once wondered after your name until today. Is that terribly cold of me?"

"Probably."

He raised a brow, the corner of his mouth quirking into an almost-grin, then dropped his cigarette and stepped on it. "Shall I guess your name, then?"

"You couldn't."

"It doesn't suit you?"

I shrugged. "Maybe it does. You can call me Mori."

"Ah, but that's not your actual name." Sherlock leaned back against the closest post and looked up at the bandstand's concave ceiling. "Is it short for something?"

"Yes, but does it really matter? Isn't Mori enough?"

Sherlock continued his study of the space above our heads. "Short for what?"

"Moriarty," I said with a sigh. I didn't have it in me to play his game that night. "And, before you ask, that is my surname. My given name is James."

"James Moriarty."

"It's a family name, and I don't want to talk about it."

"Not Jaime or something more feminine?"

I stared at him silently.

"Yes, as you said. It's a fault of mine, always wanting to get to the truth of the matter." He said it as though he didn't think it was a fault in the slightest. "But surely there must be a story."

"Really? *Sherlock* wishes to discuss odd names with me?"

"And a point to Miss Moriarty."

"Must everything be scored?" I asked, though it's possible I preened a bit internally. "Could we not merely be two strangers introducing ourselves in the park?"

"You started it."

I held back a laugh but not my smile. "You're an idiot. Truly."

Sherlock smiled widely, and it changed his whole face. He looked much younger when he smiled. "No one's ever called me that." He stared down at the ground, still smiling, like he was suddenly self-conscious. "That's not the truth. My brother, Mycroft, uses the word 'intolerable,' but I think perhaps the meaning's the same."

"Your brother is named Mycroft?"

"Yes, James. Yes, he is."

I made a face but refrained from rolling my eyes. "Did your mother despise you both from birth? Honestly."

His smile dropped. "No, she did not."

I was amazed at how quickly his mood shifted from a

rather awkward warmth to cool indifference, and again at how guilty I felt for saying the thing that set him off. I hardly knew this boy. I really shouldn't have minded his moods. He stared out over the water, just as I had done before, and his fingers fidgeted in the pocket of his long wool coat. But then he pursed his lips and stood upright. "Come along, then. I've something to show you."

"I have to get back. My brothers."

He started walking toward the path as if he hadn't heard my protest. "You'll want to see this," he called over his shoulder.

Inexplicably, I followed him. Maybe it was because I was curious what someone like Sherlock would think I'd want to see. Maybe it was because he made me smile on a "Memories of You" night. Mostly, it was because I didn't want to go home.

Chapter 4

Sherlock's long strides made it difficult for me to catch up to him but he never slowed, nor did he look back to see if I was there, not even when his path took us across Longbridge and up toward the zoo. I caught him before the circle of police tape came into view, however, and then stopped when we were still a ways from it.

"Really? We're to be gawkers at a crime scene? This is what you thought I couldn't miss?"

"We'll not be mere gawkers." He kept walking, so I was forced to jog to catch him. "We will observe."

"Semantics," I insisted, following him into the trees that grew thicker as we progressed.

"No." He turned on me, pointing back to where a growing crowd gathered at the perimeter. "Those people come to see a spectacle. I come for a purely intellectual pursuit."

I glanced around us. "My father is police."

"Police?" He briefly studied my face, as if checking to make sure I had the mark. "Everything about you is a surprise."

"That's what it means to be a stranger."

He tilted his head so that I couldn't see his eyes in the sporadic lights that filtered through the trees from the crime scene to where we stood. "Perhaps. But then I've met so few strangers in my life."

I let that go for expediency, and because I was sure the more he spoke, the more home would seem preferable to his exasperating eccentricities. "Whatever. I can't be seen here."

"Then you will not be seen." He leaned forward to meet my eyes in a challenge and turned to resume his trek.

I had no excuse for catching up with him and every excuse to walk the other way. The futures that played through my mind all seemed to end with my father's livid ranting and my apologies, but I followed Sherlock's circuitous route, deeper into the shadows toward the far end of the crime scene. I hated myself for following, but I did it. Still, the third time his route took us through a bush that smacked at my shins, I gave in to my impulse to growl at him.

"For someone who doesn't want to be seen, you make an awful lot of noise."

I glared at the back of his head but said nothing more. For a minute or so. I had just decided to complain about how far we'd wandered from the actual scene when Sherlock crouched down next to a tree and peered around it. I walked up behind him with my hands on my hips.

"What now?"

"Now," he whispered, "I will wait for the constable, who is not twenty feet away from us, to light his next cigarette, and we will sneak across while his eyes are still affected by the brightness of the flame."

I refused to crouch down, but I did step closer to him to make sure I was well hidden. Sherlock stood too and, without a word, grabbed the sleeve of my coat to pull me along behind him. We wove through the trees, then around the back of the crime-tape circle, but that apparently wasn't close enough for Sherlock. Before I could stop him, he had slipped under the tape. Once more, I followed him, this time into a life of crime, as I was pretty sure it was against the law to breach a crime scene. I knew we had come to the spot Sherlock had in mind when he stopped short and sank into the shadows between two trees.

I glanced at the scene, which was no more than a bunch of men in suits and uniforms, with booties over their shoes, wandering around and taking photos. One of the men popped up from behind an open umbrella holding a poofy black fingerprint brush and frowning. He tossed the brush into his kit and picked up the umbrella, which was glossy wet, despite the lack of rain, and had a gash in the top. He closed the umbrella and started wrestling it into a giant plastic sack, revealing a man's body behind him, slumped into a pool of blood that stained the ground beneath a tree.

It occurred to me that I should probably be shocked or repulsed at the sight—or, at least, should compose my face to appear so—but when I looked over at Sherlock, he didn't seem to be much bothered either. In fact, yet another version of the boy came out while he studied the scene of the crime.

He appeared much older, his eyes keen and focused, shifting up and down and side to side. It was as if he were painting the view with his gaze, carefully, so as not to miss a spot. I thought perhaps I even saw a bit of color in his cheeks as he worked.

"Do you see it?" he asked me in a soft whisper.

I tried to see whatever "it" was, but all I saw was the body, and the only odd bit of the body was how the man was slumped over on his side. There was something about that . . . awkward, like he hadn't tried to brace the fall.

I knew nothing about solving crimes. I'd only ever associated that kind of work with my father, and we had never really gotten on, even before he became . . . this. But perhaps there wasn't any real trick to it after all. I supposed solving one thing was nearly like solving another. And if there was one thing I was good at, it was solving for X.

I decided to think of the crime as the steps in an equation, to sort how he could have fallen into that position. Equations were easy. Put a pin into each of the things you know and then write rules between the pins, like strings, connecting one pin to the next until you can solve for the missing parts. But in this instance, I couldn't seem to move along the string of the first unknown. After all, if what my father had said was right and the man did die the evening before, the bigger question was why in the world he would've wandered into the darkest part of the park at night. There was nothing to see where we stood. And while there was no bench where he fell, there was one just a few trees away, where a lamp would have offered some light.

I counted off the steps, starting with the man running from something. He could have seen his attacker coming and hoped to find a place to hide in the dark. But that didn't fit either, because of the way the body was positioned. It was as though he'd been leaning casually against the tree, and just slumped down and then teetered over. If he'd been running away, he'd have been tackled, sprawled out on the ground, not slumped. I started again with him running and hiding, somehow getting backed up against the tree. But even trapped, he would have tried to block the attacker with his hands. I tried to find his hands, to see if there were cuts or some other sign of his fighting back. I even traced the angles of his arm to a bright, golden watch, but that hand was tucked away. So was his other hand. His hands were still in his pockets.

I had no idea that was even possible, for a man to die with his hands in his pockets. It meant he couldn't have known he was being killed until the wound was already in his chest.

When I started my equation again, I had a few important pins. The dead man trusted his killer to get close and personal. The man had obviously come there on purpose. He wasn't afraid when he walked into the woods—into the dark to meet his fate. He leaned back against the tree, his hands in his pockets to show just how casual he felt. In contrast, his eyes were wide in death, surprised as the killer used his weapon.

"He knew the killer," I whispered to Sherlock.

"The hands," he said. It started to drizzle, and two uniformed officers carefully draped a bright-yellow tarp over the body. We'd come just in time to take our notes.

Some muttering in the crowd of police stole my attention, and the sea of suited men suddenly parted as a large, sandy-colored man with a walrus-esque figure and demeanor stomped through the scene. All the men paid him deference, with "sir" and "guv" accompanying every nod and step aside. The Walrus Man ignored them all, making a beeline for a man clutching a clipboard. "Coroner come and gone?" asked the walrus.

"Not without that." Clipboard man actually had to point out the bright-yellow tarp. My mind reeled at the lack of observance necessary to completely miss the central focus of the entire scene. That this man was apparently the senior officer forced an exasperated sound from me before I could stifle it. Sherlock tensed but didn't look at me.

"Taking his time, I see," said the walrus. "So, what've we got?"

Clipboard held an evidence bag up to the lights. "Wallet, opened and empty next to the deceased. Stab wounds. Lots of blood. It's even on his umbrella and the tree."

He was right. There was a darker patch on the tree that started just below a white gouge mark that looked wet, as wet as the umbrella, which seemed much more significant in that light.

"So, robbery gone wrong?" asked Walrus.

"Had to be something like that."

Sherlock made a sound deep in his throat that was much louder than the one I had made, and when our eyes met, I widened mine, hoping he'd take it as an invitation to shut up. Still, it was obvious even to me that this was no robbery. I mean, the watch alone—

"Maybe he was out for a run," Walrus offered.

"In wool trousers," Sherlock whispered, derisively.

"An evening constitutional," the other officer said. "That's good. I'll jot that in the report."

"All sorted, then. Good, good."

The men started down the hill toward the crowd as we backtracked toward the tape. The very moment we were out of earshot, Sherlock practically exploded with outrage.

"The incompetence! The base incompetence and absolute reckless idiocy!"

His eyes were full of fire again, and I couldn't help but notice how intriguing he looked with his eyes wider and his cheeks aflame. Passion. It had to be his passion. Everyone is infinitely more attractive when they're full of the stuff.

"Disheartening," I added to his list of adjectives as we extricated ourselves from the crime scene. "To think our safety in this park is in the hands of two—"

"Actual jackasses!" Sherlock cried. "They could place actual donkeys in uniforms and get better deduction."

"Technically, those two weren't in uniform, of course."

I smiled when Sherlock continued on as though I hadn't spoken a word. He was clearly not to be distracted from his ranting. I can't say I minded. We were taking a much more direct route back to the park's inner circle path.

"The noises of beasts, Mori! I would listen to pack animals heaving out calls deep into the night before I'd lower myself to listen to even one more syllable."

I took his hand in mine and tried my best to repress a laugh when that simple action quieted him almost instantly. I'd done it without thinking, really, like I would to my brothers when they were younger and would be on about something. Sherlock stared down at our joined hands, then up at my face.

"Are you done?" I asked.

Sherlock sighed. "Probably." A wry grin lifted his cheeks. He squeezed my hand gently, and then fidgeted a bit as we walked. Once we reached the path, he swung our hands a little, like he wasn't able to hold still. "Or perhaps not." He released my hand and turned toward me. "We should take the case."

"'Take the case'?" I wanted to laugh openly at him then. "Do you think at all before you speak?"

"We could do it. We are clever. The swans on the lake are more clever than those detectives. Perhaps even the trees."

"Yes, yes. They were morons. But it's not as though we are a part of the investigation. How do you propose we learn anything at all about the crime or who did it or why?"

"Observation. Deduction. Sheer mind power."

"And when we've nothing left to observe?"

"You said your dad is police."

"He doesn't even want me in the park right now. He would definitely not be okay with my investigating a murder."

"So, you think it's more than just a mugging gone wrong?"

I pursed my lips.

"As do I," he added hastily. "And with your cleverness and my reasoning, we could come up with an answer well before the police."

"For what purpose?"

Sherlock offered me a half smile before he said, "Because we can."

It was a very infectious smile. "You think I am merely clever?"

He shrugged. "I don't know you that well. Not yet."

I shook my head. "'Because we can' isn't good enough."

Sherlock stepped closer. "How about we make this a bit of a game?"

I tried to roll my eyes and act like I wasn't completely intrigued, but I was a piss-poor actor on a good day, despite my years in drama. "Go on."

"First one to solve the crime, wins."

"Wins what?"

"Wins the game."

"And what will be the rules?"

"No rules," he said.

"All games have rules."

"Fine. The only rule is total transparency. We must both know what the other knows." I started to respond to that, but as usual, Sherlock interrupted. "But not tonight. I need some time to think." He lit a cigarette and stared past me. I got the feeling he was already walking away from me in his mind. "Tomorrow after your play practice. My lab."

He started to walk, and it was all I could do to keep a growl out of my voice when I answered his summons. "No."

Sherlock turned, surprised. "No?"

I shook my head. "No, I haven't decided whether I want

to play or not. And besides, if I do decide to be part of this insanity, no one can know I'm part of this. I'm serious. If my dad finds out, I'm screwed." I looked around and saw the lake off in the distance. "If I decide to play, we'll meet here. At the dock. We'll take a boat out and that way no one can overhear, and it won't smell of burning dust and spilled fake blood."

Sherlock's lips tightened and then stretched in a grin. "How do you know it's fake?"

He didn't wait for an answer. He was already striding off when I thought of one.

Chapter 5

I was halfway through the next morning before I came out of my Sherlock fog and decided that I was definitely NOT going to play his little game. Unfortunately, Sherlock most likely wouldn't be anywhere I could find him until after school. Not that it mattered. I was resolved. Mostly.

My family ate breakfast in silence, the five of us, Dad crunching his bran while the rest of us slurped oatmeal. None of us made eye contact or even shifted in our seats until Dad was off to work, without a word about his day or ours. I grabbed Sean's chin and tilted his face up toward the light.

"Is it covered?" he asked.

I'd practically plastered his face with concealer to cover the bruise from the night before. It was hard to blend it all in with his baby skin, though. "As best I could."

"Enough to fool the Benz?" Michael asked.

Sean's teacher was Miss Benson. She'd been at the grammar school long enough to have taught each of us in her class. Nothing fooled the Benz.

"If she asks, you say . . ." I let go of Sean's chin and took my dishes to the sink, where Freddie was washing up.

"My brothers and I were arsing—"

"Mucking," I corrected.

"Yeah. Mucking about."

Freddie laughed. "Say 'arsing' to the Benz. I dare ya."

Sean chucked the crust of his toast at Freddie, which would have devolved into a free-for-all dishwater/food fight had I not fired off a glare for each of them. "Quit it and make your lunches or you'll starve and deserve it."

I threw a final glare over my shoulder before I left for school, just for good measure, but I was pretty sure the squeal I heard when I was halfway down the street came from my house.

Much of my school day was spent rehearsing what I would say to Sherlock when he asked me to be a part of his "investigation." But nothing I came up with adequately made the point that I wasn't *afraid* to play the game, I was merely uninterested. That I had even entertained the idea for a second showed just how that ridiculous Holmes boy had managed to mess with my mind in ways he shouldn't have been able. Sherlock was trouble. Unexpected. And by the time I got to drama, I'd decided that *I* didn't have to come up with any kind of explanation. I hardly knew the boy.

I shouldn't have been surprised to see him suddenly appear backstage halfway through my class, but there he was, waiting in the wings, waving at me as I fumbled through my lines. When I didn't immediately heed his unspoken call, he started pacing the boards, glancing up impatiently at me every thirty seconds or so. At one point, I thought he might actually come out onto the stage to fetch me. Luckily, my scene ended before he could.

He opened his mouth to speak as I approached, and I held up my hand to stop him. Surprisingly, it worked. "What are you doing here?" I whispered.

"I need to tell you something. It couldn't wait."

"It can wait." I grabbed his arm and tugged toward the back exit. "It will wait."

"Don't be ridiculous." Sherlock straightened the sleeve of his uniform when I let go. "If it wasn't important, I wouldn't be here. But we must talk to her. Right away. It's vital."

"Talk to whom?"

Sherlock gestured at my dress. "Her. The one you're replacing."

I copied his gesture, exasperated. "She is obviously not here, or I wouldn't be replacing her today."

His countenance fell. "Her name is Patel, yes?"

"Sure. Lily Patel. Why? What is so vital about talking to Lily?"

"Her dad," Sherlock said. "The body in the park was her dad."

I somehow managed to shoo Sherlock out of the theater with promises to keep our meet-up at the boat dock. At that point, I was so desperate to rid myself of him that I would've agreed to meet him in the Queen's bedchambers had he asked. But his revelation changed things a bit for me. The crime was more immediate. Closer. The pieces were in reach, not far flung and remote. Instead of continuing to obsess over a way out of the game, I was suddenly focused completely on Lily Patel and how I could manage to question her without seeming to. Of course, I wished to do it in a way that wouldn't also escalate her grief, but that wasn't top priority.

A mostly simple plan unfolded in my mind, starting with finding out where she lived. I was still backstage, surrounded by side-stage draping, stagehands, and costumed classmates. I grabbed the arm of the next person who rushed past me and tried to remember if I'd ever heard Lily's boyfriend's name. I was pretty sure I'd never written it down, or I'd remember for sure. I knew he was in this course. It was John something or other—

"Watkins?" I said as a question to the arm I'd grabbed. I was hoping the arm's owner would point me in the right direction and maybe even confirm that was the boyfriend's name. Turns out I had unfortunate luck.

He scowled. "I'm Watson. But I prefer John, if it's all the same. Let go of my arm."

I wasn't entirely sure this Watson was the one, so I said, "The bloke Lily dates. You remember his name?"

John's eyes narrowed and he pulled his arm from my grasp. "What do you want with her?"

"I don't want anything with her. At present, I want to know the name of her boy."

John sighed and shook his head. "I'll give you a hint: His name isn't Watkins."

"It's you, then?"

He seemed to grow more suspicious with my smile, so I dropped it. "What do you want with her?"

"Nothing, I said. It's just that . . . well, I've just heard about her dad."

"That's none of your business." He started to walk away, which sent my mind spinning for a way to stop him.

"Wait." I didn't mean to grab his arm, but he was forced to pull free again, this time stepping out of my reach and deepening his frown. I was evidently rubbish at getting information out of people. "No, I know. I just felt I should give my condolences or something. I mean, we've been in school a few years together."

John's expression melted into either mild distrust or acute wariness, whichever kept his eyebrows from sinking permanently into the cavernous wrinkle at the bridge of his nose. "Yeah, well, I'll tell her."

"I'd like to tell her myself," I said quickly. "Will she be back to school soon?"

He shook his head. "Not for a while yet."

"Will there be a memorial?"

He stared at me through his bangs with pursed lips. I stared back. "Saturday. Two p.m."

Chapter 6

The rest of drama practically dragged on forever. I couldn't seem to sit still out in the audience, like I normally would've, watching as each of those students wanting to be graded as a director ran a scene, none of which included Lily's character. My attempts at standing side stage quickly turned into a kind of rocking, twisting dance that irritated even myself. At last, I gave up and took to pacing behind the backdrop curtain, until I spotted a rodent-type animal that looked at me in a rather threatening way as I neared it. I tried glaring back, but it stood its ground until I was obviously forced to spin around and flee with my life.

Rodents. Horrible, pointless things.

Finally, the bell rang, and it was all I could do not to rip the costume from my body the minute I got into the dressing room. No idea why it was suddenly so urgent for me to be at the Regent's Park boat dock with the speed of the demons. Thankfully, I caught myself before I got too near and was able to slow my pace to a disinterested stroll. Just because I had some sort of news didn't at all mean that I would be joining Sherlock's game.

Or tell him about it.

"You're here," he announced as I walked up.

"I promised."

"Yes, well, promises, in my experience, mean very little. Still, well done."

Honestly, he was the most infuriating, condescending, ridiculous—

"Shall we?" He waved toward the little boathouse, ignorant of my internal ranting.

He seemed twitchy as we walked. He kept taking turns staring at the path ahead and down at my hand. This left me feeling more than a little self-conscious about my bloody hand of all things. I kept wondering what he was seeing, what scar or smudge or chip in my polish would give him insight into my heritage, personality, or personal grooming habits.

About the time I expected him to declare that I had eaten salmon last Wednesday and would become an ardent Catholic in my seventies, I decided that this "observe and judge" quirk was his most irritating quality. I sighed and was just about to ask him what on earth was so damned fascinating about my hand when he reached across the gap between us and took it in his. He instantly calmed, and, despite my surprise, I felt my own inner tension soothe as well. I even smiled a bit. There was something wretchedly endearing about Sherlock's manner. Even when he was irritating.

He, of course, had no idea what to do with my hand once he held it, and quickly returned to his twitchy ways. Luckily, I had only a few steps left to tolerate his grasping and swinging until we reached the window outside the café, where boats could be rented. All the while, I was determined not to acknowledge the familiarity I felt when we were together. I sometimes wasn't sure if I was compensating for his awkwardness, or if this strange boy actually made me feel . . . whatever it was that makes one feel at home with a stranger. Like I'd known him forever.

As payback for this inner treachery, I made him struggle for almost a full minute with trying to remove his ID and money from his wallet one-handed before letting go of his hand, a thought that clearly hadn't occurred to him.

Our boat was a blue fiberglass thing with a light wood floor, two blue benches, and orange oars. Number 28.

"Any thoughts on our case?" he asked, once we were out on the water.

I, in fact, had many, but I covered with, "You first."

"How shall we start our little game?"

"I'm not sure I want to play yet."

His eyes practically lit up with the news. "Oh, well. I can't blame you for being intimidated, having so much less experience with these things."

"Oh? Solved a lot of crimes, have you?"

That was evidently the exact right thing to say. I hated how much he was enjoying this. "I meant with deductive reasoning. The crime is incidental to the puzzle."

"Our schoolmate's father is dead, but, yes—incidental."

He shrugged off my sarcasm. "Still, I'll understand if—"

I knew what he was doing. He couldn't have been more

obvious, and still I interrupted his smug ridiculousness with, "You worry about you. I'll worry about me."

I watched as his lip twitched, but he managed to suppress whatever expression might have escaped. "I thought you weren't going to play."

"I'm not."

"Then why are you here?"

"I thought you should know there's to be a memorial. Tomorrow at two. I'm invited."

He couldn't have known it was a lie, no matter how high his brows raised after I'd said it.

"You may tag along if you'd like."

I was pretty sure that his next expression was mocking, but he only said, "How kind of you."

"So . . ." I looked out over the lake and watched the swans for a bit.

"We should probably get started."

"And how would we do that?" I tried to act bored, and then added, "Were I to decide to play along. Which I haven't yet."

"As you said."

My expression dared him to comment further. He did not. He was perhaps wiser than first impressions would indicate.

"We should probably recognize up front that this will likely be some sort of mundane puzzle."

"Why?"

"Because most puzzles are horribly mundane."

"Then why bother?"

"Because until we have the data to prove otherwise, there is still the possibility that it will fascinate."

"And what's so fascinating about a stabbing in the park? I'm sure they happen all the time."

I knew the answer, of course. I knew it before he smirked and leaned in closer than I would have preferred. I could have mouthed the words as he spoke them.

"His hands were in his pockets."

The one clue that shouldn't have meant anything, yet meant everything, because it didn't make any sense at all. "It's impossible." I'd spoken aloud unintentionally, and couldn't seem to stop once I'd started. "There must be some alternative explanation. Perhaps the killer put his hands back in his pockets after the fact. It has to be something like that."

"Why in the world would he do it? There's no reason."

"But it has to be," I countered. "There isn't a single scenario where a person being attacked would leave his hands in his pockets."

"If the killer was very close before he pulled out the knife, maybe Patel didn't see it."

"After he was stabbed, then. It takes less than a second to rip your hands from your pockets. He would have tried to cover the wound. It's in our nature to do it, even when we're too late to stop the knife and it's useless to stop the bleeding. We try. Until our last breath, we try."

Sherlock studied my face. Again. But I wasn't willing to leave my train of thought, not even to indulge my irritation.

"It's impossible. I mean, the man would have to have been

dead almost the second the knife entered his body, and . . . oh."
I let the scene play out once more in my mind, the same that
had played as I looked at the tarp-covered body that night
in the park. At the blood on the tree, which had been at the
man's back. At the umbrella, which hadn't been his at all. "If it
pierced through to mark the tree, it wasn't a knife."

"A sword, then? But if you don't buy him hiding a knife
until the last minute, how exactly would he hide the length
of a sword?"

"Perhaps along the handle of—"

Sherlock's brow cleared before I could finish my thought,
and he stood up, swaying the boat rather dangerously. "The
umbrella!" he cried out. Half the lake was staring at us by the
time I pulled him back down to his bench. "We're brilliant
at this."

I refused to smile as I put my ideas together aloud. "If he
was pierced through to the wood of the tree."

"If it pierced through his heart and his spine."

"If that could even be done with any length of sword
without the man lifting his hands from his pockets."

"It was dark," Sherlock offered. "And perhaps it was a short
sword."

"Tantó," I said, at the same time Sherlock said, "Gladius!"

"Roman," Sherlock offered.

I countered with, "Japanese. Ten inches long, super sharp,
and used in martial arts for demonstrations."

"Ancient, two feet long, and most likely less widely avail-
able. You win." Sherlock scowled. "It's no good, though.

47

Those things are all illegal. How would our killer get his hands on a sword, short or not? There probably isn't a single one in London that isn't under lock and key in some museum or historical society."

He was right, of course, but wrong at the same time, because I knew of at least one such sword in London. It was up in our attic, without a lock or key to speak of. That is, if Dad hadn't found it and tossed it by now. I even remembered the day my mother showed me where she kept it, in the shadows of one of the beams, where no one would think to look, she said. My mother had endless secrets. She loved to tell them to me, and still it felt like I'd never come close to knowing anything really important about her. That was what she was like. She made you feel like you knew what no one else did, but really it was something useless, like where the sword was hidden.

"Besides, they'll never look in a copper's house for illegal booty," she had said. She was running her aikido forms, one hand holding the sword over her head, parallel to the roof. She held the position for one perfectly still moment, then sliced the sword through the air, impaling an invisible opponent in the neck behind her, before spinning to stab him again through the heart. For just that next moment, she was ferocious, deadly. I could believe she was a warrior—capable of anything.

But then she glanced from her ghostly opponent to me and winked. She was my mum again, and when she smiled, every trace of the warrior was gone.

"There are loads of weapons in the city," I told Sherlock,

deciding he didn't need to know about Mum's sword. "You know someone's got one that was handed down to him from a family member or something."

He seemed to consider what I said, then dismissed it with a shake of his head.

I shrugged. "It could have been any kind of long dagger. But do you think it's possible to pierce a man through like that?" I followed my mother's forms in my mind again and superimposed that over the crime scene, until they became one in my mind. Because if the killer had his back to Patel . . . "One to paralyze and one to kill him before he can even lift his hands to defend himself. Could the body have had two wounds?"

He frowned. "Possible. But why two?"

"One through the throat, which, if it cut into the spine, would stop movement to the hands."

"And kill him just the same."

"But what if it didn't? What if the first missed the brain stem, the part that would kill a man instantly, but severed the spine in such a way that it created a C4 injury, so that he was left gasping and paralyzed. How high was the gash in the tree?"

Sherlock nodded. "Yes. It was high up—perhaps too high for a thrust to Patel's chest. Though I couldn't see a second gash from where we were. But the blood could have obscured a second wound, yes?"

"What if the killer really knew aikido? What if he was following a form he'd learned with a sword in class?" Without

49

thinking, I lifted my arm over my head, holding an invisible sword just as my mom had. "Do you think we could have a trained assassin . . . ?"

I let the ridiculous suggestion hang in the air before scowling at my own words. Sherlock seemed overly pleased by it, however.

"You tell me," he said.

"If I knew, I would not have asked the question." It would seem that every time I momentarily forgot how infuriating Sherlock was, he found a new way to remind me.

Sherlock's lips twitched before he spoke. "You obviously have some kind of martial arts experience."

"Took aikido classes with my mom when I was a kid, which I'm sure doesn't count as—"

"I take boxing. And fencing. We're quite the army, you and I."

I started to correct him, but I was pretty sure Sherlock didn't hear over the high-pitched wailing sound of his mobile ringing. He pulled it out and rolled his eyes at whatever he'd seen on the screen before answering, "I'm busy."

I looked out across the lake, but the tightness in the way Sherlock said, "I see," got my attention. He turned his face away from me before I could find his expression.

"Of course. I'll be home within the hour."

He didn't speak to me the entire way back to the dock, not even an answer when I offered to help him row, and when he finally faced me, he wasn't sad or angry or cold. He just looked like he was about to ask me some deep, dark question.

Only he never asked. He did offer a hand to help me out of the boat. He even mumbled something about seeing me back to my house. And when I offered to stand in line to return the oars to the rental window so he could go, he merely nodded and wandered away from the café. Which is why I was so surprised to see him just around the bend waiting for me when I was done.

"You didn't need to stay. I know you have somewhere to be."

I might as well have spoken to the bench across the way. Sherlock didn't even move.

"You should go. I can find my way home."

Still nothing.

I toyed with the idea of waving a hand in front of his face, but decided to just let him be, and wandered back out of the park on my own. I did look back once, however, and watched him look around briefly for me, before he shoved his hands into his pockets, shrugged, and started down my same path.

I wondered if I'd ever get a glimpse inside that mind of his. Then I quickly shuddered at the very desire.

Chapter 7

I woke up Saturday morning facing the wrong direction. I'd had the dream again, the one where the past six months have been the nightmare and my mom's really alive—that I could see her again, if I could just get downstairs for breakfast. Only, in the dream, everything goes wrong. The shower won't work, my closet's empty of clothes, and I can't find the door to the stairs. Dream Me starts to panic, desperate to see my mother and never able to reach her. Before I can, I wake up and the dream fades away completely.

But the feeling of her being in the house stays, so that for one waking moment, I think she's still alive.

After three mornings of that, I had placed the program from her memorial service on my nightstand, so it would be the first thing I saw when I woke up. Dreams are so cruel. I never wanted to believe in them when awake. Not even for a moment.

But that morning, the morning of Lily's dad's memorial, I woke up looking the wrong way, and by the time I saw the program, I was wrecked. I waded through the day in a fog of the dream. Not even the electric tension of the boys cooped up in the house could distract me from that feeling of being on the edge of a cliff, on the verge of losing my grip. Like a feather's weight might be enough to send me hurtling down.

At lunch, I caught myself expecting Mum to walk through the door, and barely escaped out to our front steps in time to keep the boys from seeing my breakdown. I stared at the sky, my chest heaving and my eyes flooding beyond my control. I focused on my breathing, on the scared look Michael gave me the first time he caught me crying over Mum, on how embarrassed I'd be if Sherlock walked up while I was so emotional. When neither worked, I thought of all her things, those few I'd managed to pilfer from Dad's collection, hidden under my bed—the pictures, the letters, the coin.

The coin was just an oversize gold-painted novelty with a four-leaf clover on one side and a tree on the other—the kind with Celtic knots sprouting from the branches and falling down to entwine with the roots below. She used to flip the coin across the tops of her fingers and back, a nervous habit she only ever indulged on those rare occasions when Dad wasn't around. Not that he was always home. He had this way of feeling present even when he was gone. And we could never count on him to stay that way. He'd show up at odd times and hours, like we could never really know his schedule. He lingered.

The day I asked Mum to teach me how to flip the coin like she did, she'd instead taught me how to palm the coin and make it disappear. It took two more days for me to learn to walk the coin between my fingers and flip it to my palm first, and when I'd mastered that, she gave me the coin to keep.

"Keep it in a secret place, Mori," she'd said. "This is just between you and me, yeah?"

"A secret?" I had whispered.

Mum had smiled and looked around us before leaning close to whisper back. "People who share a secret are bound together forever, but only if they keep it."

I'd nodded and smiled and felt very grown up, to have a secret with my mum against the world. And she'd said forever, not just for life, so I supposed we were still bonded. I swiped my eyes and slumped down onto the steps of our front stoop. I'd never told anyone about the coin—never even showed it to the boys. I heard them thunder through the house, one of them screaming at the other, a sure sign Dad was at work. Another wave of pain swept over me, and I stared out at the cars surging past to distract me from it.

Soon, the white noise of traffic blurred things enough for me to go back in. I dressed quickly and escaped once more to the streets. Sherlock waited for me on the sidewalk, greeting me with only a nod. I didn't feel like being around him just then, but I'd promised to take him to the memorial, and I would. Still, I didn't talk during our walk to the Tube, and he seemed okay with that. Sherlock appeared lost in thoughts of his own, really.

"Is everything all right?"

Sherlock forced a grin. "What could be wrong?"

And that was the extent of our conversation for the whole of the trip to Mr. Patel's memorial.

The parish was a drab yellowish brick on the outside, but the chapel was beautiful. Giant white columns stood ominously in all four corners of the room. A chandelier hung low enough to create a spiderweb shadow across the parquet floor of the main aisle, the sparkle of the glass ornamentation competing with the various stained-glass windows to welcome in the afternoon sun.

But despite all the formality of the decor, the service itself was quite casual, an odd mix of Mr. Patel's Hindu tradition and their family's Protestant beliefs. All the people on the left side of the chapel were dressed in white, and took turns draping the stage and urn with garlands of flowers. A man in white linen robes called speakers up by name, each of whom shared an anecdote that either caused their own tears to spill or earned a sobbed laugh from Mrs. Patel, Lily's mother. We were seated with the rest of Lily's school friends, on the opposite side of the chapel in the second row, so I had a direct line of sight to Lily—her mother on one side, her Watson on the other. Lily sat still, her eyes glued to the large printed photo of her father that stood in the corner.

I remembered that stillness.

Lily's mom cried freely, her gaze only rising to the photo twice through the whole service, each time with a slight wince, like someone had pricked her with a pin. There was something completely familiar in her mannerisms. She would rest her tissue-clad hands in her lap, and then scoot them up to her knees. Down at her sides, crossing her chest, then remembering herself and letting them fall to her lap once again. She was lost. She didn't even know what to do with her own body anymore.

It had been the same with my dad. He couldn't sit still at our mom's memorial either. But not all spouses acted that way.

I'd spent an entire month of Saturdays after my mom passed attending various advertised memorials, just to study the mourners—to figure out how I was supposed to be feeling, or maybe acting. Because all I felt was numb—a numbness I knew showed on my face and in my every movement.

I'd seen loads of women who sat with a quiet strength, the tears in their eyes never falling throughout the service. Some seemed disconnected from the service entirely, as if wandering through the secret rooms of their mind, thinking things we'd never discover. I even saw one woman who whimpered through the entire service, held up on all sides by grandchildren. I watched as she reached out and petted each of their ginger heads in turn, and how they snuggled closer to her at the contact. I remembered thinking I would have been the one grandchild to scoot away from them all, separate myself, not wanting to be touched. Not that my grandmother would have dared touch me.

My earliest memories are of grandparents. Not mine, but I suppose they had to be somebody's. My grandparents moved across England like it was their job to live-test as many houses as they could before they died. I couldn't blame them for hating their houses enough to want an escape. Their lives were so noxious, they'd probably escape their own skin if they could. Unfortunately, they kept escaping that toxic together, and it was the together that made their homes so toxic.

Instead of blaming each other, they blamed the houses, even when it meant hemorrhaging their fortune in fees and underwater mortgages or abandoning an unsellable cottage to the elements. My mother left at age fifteen, when the money ran out and they were forced to live in a tight little row house on Baker Street—our house now, as it turned out. Her sister, my aunt Lucia, escaped into a hateful marriage of her own only to return when her husband ran off to Austria or Australia or somewhere else that started with an *A*.

My memories, though, are of someone else's grandparents—the kind who live out in the countryside. Cornwall, perhaps. They both had long, flowing white hair, hers kinked with a natural curl, his spreading down his cheeks to cover his chin. Their house was blue, and the backyard lush and green with grass and fruit trees and giant garden plants that reached for the sun from soil so rich it looked black.

I'd toddled along the tiny path that allowed them to tend their plants, and they'd picked ripe fruit and vegetables for me to taste test. I remembered liking the tomatoes and strawberries best. I'd also liked when they looked from me to each other, and then moved to hold one another around their waists, as if there were magnets in their loose-fitting gardening trousers. Magnets that only attracted each other. Magnets that didn't let go, even when I ran up to show them a ladybug or flower blossom I'd discovered in the shadows under the leaves.

My parents had magnets as well. Not the kind that fit together with a gentle click, more the kind that pulled and strained until one side or the other was yanked savagely back into place with a large thunk that sent shock waves through them both. I do believe they loved each other, just not in that gentle, peaceful way the grandparents in the garden had discovered. My parents loved each other with blustering rows and stormy silences. They did nothing halfway, nothing subtle. They wrapped around each other to kiss in the kitchen, wrestled around the living room screaming with laughter, and fought so loudly, only his badge kept them both from being hauled away on a domestic.

As loud as they were, I don't remember a single word they said in those fights. Only the noise. Now our house was always quiet. Us tiptoeing our way around the sleeping, sobbing giant in the corner room. Him brooding and grunting and hiding himself away from us. I sometimes wonder if he misses the noise like I do.

I wondered if Lily's house was quiet now too. I wondered if Mrs. Patel still felt the pull of a magnet buried under six feet of earth.

"What do you see?" Sherlock breathed into my ear.

I shook my head in answer, but I knew he wouldn't leave it alone, so I excused myself and sidestepped my way out of the pew to escape down the far aisle. The back of the chapel felt like another world. A collage of pictures was spread about a table, snapshots of Lily's dad with his family through the years.

He hadn't lived a very posh life, but he'd had a lot of friends and had done a lot with them. There were pictures of them sitting around a fire pit smoking, basking in the sun on a canal boat, bundled up for some snowshoeing. By the time I reached the far end of the table, my gaze was skimming around the remaining pictures, looking for something of interest—something to give me pause.

I found it.

My mother's face, younger and smiling brightly for the camera, flashed out at me from the sea of faces. I didn't believe my own eyes at first—what with the way this whole day had pointed me to her memory. But when I looked away and looked back, she was still there. When I lifted the snapshot from the table, she was still there, the arm of some bloke I'd never seen in my life around her shoulders, her arm around the waist of a woman with bright blue hair, and Mr. Patel standing behind three other men.

Before I could study it more, I heard footsteps approaching and slid the picture into my handbag, pulling out a tissue in the same movement in case I was seen. I swept the tissue across my dry eyes and used the ruse to search the rest of the pictures for another glimpse of my mother's face. But there were no more of her.

"He certainly lived a full life." A white-haired woman reached out to pat my back, and I realized just in time that I was meant to be crying over these memories, that crying people were meant to be grateful for a pat on the back from a stranger, not repelled by it.

I nodded and let my hair fall down to mask my tearless face. "Yes."

"We're glad of that. After all the troubles of his youth, we weren't sure he wouldn't have ended up locked away. A life wasted that would've been."

I was pretty sure there wasn't strictly a "we" involved in this gossip-filled concern, but Mr. Patel's troubled youth was exactly when he had known my mom, and I was desperate to learn more about that. "Troubled?"

"Aye," she said, patting my back with more vigor as she leaned in to drop her voice even lower. "In with a wrong crowd. I trust you won't be doing the same?"

I risked a glance and caught the woman searching the table.

"I could have sworn there was a photo here," she muttered. "Female at the center of it all."

"A girl?"

The woman clicked her tongue and sighed. "Ah, but there always is. And this one had the face of a cherub. On the street she was the picture of innocent beauty, but inside lived a wolf." The woman shifted her gaze to my face before I could cover with the tissue. "Ah, there now." She paused. "You look a bit like her, you know."

Her gaze dropped to the table, and I shot a look over my shoulder. People started to rise from their pews, including Sherlock, who was beelining through the crowd for me.

"If I could just find the photo, I'd show you."

"I've got to go," I mumbled, stepping into the first surge of people making their way out front. I spilled out onto the street and turned back just as John Watson was walking a stiff, unemotive Lily away from the chapel. Her mother stared after her but quickly turned back to greet the attendees.

"Well, this was a waste of time," Sherlock pronounced from his sudden appearance at my side.

I frowned and started to walk in the opposite direction of John and Lily, toward our Tube entrance.

"Do I take from your silence that you learned something?"

"There is always something to learn," I said.

Sherlock pulled out a cigarette and lit up. I felt my scowl deepen.

"Not here. Just a bunch of stories, most of which are likely fiction, meant to show the dead man to be far greater than he was. Typical." He took a deep drag and blew it out to the sky.

I stopped walking. In my mind, he kept walking without me, beating me to the station so that I could take a different train. In my mind, he evaporated so that I could be alone with the picture of my mother, free to study it at my leisure without his prying eyes. No one ever does what I want.

"What is it?" His eyes brightened as they met mine. "You know something! Tell. It's the rules."

I shook my head. "Don't get your hopes high. It's nothing a quick search wouldn't have uncovered."

I paused but was too distracted to think of something to tell him. I was determined not to touch my handbag, or look at it too much. Then again, I didn't want to be seen to avoid it. And the more these directives spiraled around my mind, the fewer ideas I had for some great reveal. In the end, I said, "I just heard a bit of gossip, which may not be true. But this woman said Mr. Patel had been in trouble when he was a kid."

"What kind of trouble?"

"She made it sound like his trouble was with the police."

The light left Sherlock's eyes and he took another long drag from his cigarette, and then tossed it into the gutter. "Nothing of note. Still, a wasted day."

I didn't know why his declaration upset me like it did, but I couldn't even speak to him after that. I took perhaps too much time to offer him a directed glare, and then I stormed down the road, leaving him the way I'd just wished he would leave me.

Unfortunately, I stormed in a direction opposite the train and ended up walking the six blocks to the stop at Monument. It, of course, didn't have my line, so I ended up taking the bus, walking to Moorgate, and catching a late train back to our station. By the time I got to Baker Street, I could think of nothing I wanted less than to go home. I walked to the park instead, as if I were hearing its call.

I practically fell onto my beloved bandstand. I resisted the urge to crawl across it to my seat on the other side, but I was tempted. Later, I would blame the fact that I was too exhausted from the day to explain how I could fail to notice my smoking gent standing in the shadows beyond. When the scent of Sherlock's cloves finally did strike me, it sent me into the foulest of moods.

I decided to pretend he wasn't there, which worked for a while. He smoked, and I stared out across the lake, wishing the light from the rising moon would strike him into oblivion like a million bolts of lightning all at once. Violent fantasies aside, the longer we stood in silence, the less worked up I became, until finally he rubbed out the filter of his clove and walked over toward me.

"I'm sorry," he said with finality, as though his words were the solution to something and not the opening of our conversation.

I shrugged and kicked my feet out a few times, letting my heels fall back to strike against the cement with a rubbery flop.

Sherlock cleared his throat and came around to face me. "I am sorry."

I slid down from my perch so that we were eye to eye—or would've been were he not eight inches taller than me. "For what?"

He was taken aback by the question—looked almost indignant about it, really, which lightened my mood for some reason.

I said, "You don't even know what to apologize for."

I turned to go, and he stopped me with a soft, "Wait."

I met his gaze again, determined not to let him off the hook, though my anger somehow managed to evaporate for no good reason at all.

He dipped his hand into his pocket and brought out his pack of cigarettes, then thrust them back in and sighed. "It's for whatever it was I saw in your eyes before you left me at the church. I'm not sorry for saying what was obviously correct, but I am sorry for causing that."

I stared him down until he was forced to look away, which would have made me smile on any other night. How he managed to insist on his own rightness and still make me feel better, I'd never have been able to say. But he looked so handsome standing there with his hands in his pockets, his eyes open to the sky, as if the very air held answers to the question of me. I couldn't help myself. I grasped the lapels of his wool coat and drew him down so I could press a soft, chaste kiss. His struggling to free his hands made me smile against his lips. But I spun out of reach before he could hold me in place.

"What . . . ?"

I must admit watching the great mind of Sherlock Holmes struggle to ask even a single question was perhaps the best part of that wretched day. Other than the kiss itself. I caught my fingers touching my lips and turned my back to him, looking over my shoulder briefly to say, "Looked like you needed a distraction."

I walked across the lawn to the lit-up path. Listening to his hurried steps as he scrambled to catch up with me was definitely the second-best part.

Chapter 8

I had too much in my head when I went to sleep that night, and spent most of Sunday staring at the picture of Mr. Patel and Mum. I took time between homework assignments to memorize the minutiae of the background until I was sure I'd know the room they were in were I to walk into it by accident, regardless of any changes to the decor. I'd been reduced to naming the people by appearance to keep them in my head. There were seven in all—Mr. Patel, my mother, the Blue-Haired Girl, the Man in Green, Striped Man, Mustache Man, and the man with his arm around my mom, whom I called Stepdad.

When I finally went to bed Sunday night, my sleep was troubled. Each member of the snapshot played a part in my dreams, leading me down paths, promising to reveal their identities if we could just get to the paths' mythical end. I woke with the quest at the forefront of my thoughts and was so distracted, I washed my hair three times and only realized I'd forgotten to put on makeup entirely when I was most of the way to school.

It wasn't like me at all to have flitting thoughts. I was out of control. Off plan. I should've told Sherlock I wasn't interested in his little crime the very minute I discovered my mother's picture at the funeral. I should've placed the photo in my little box of my mother's things and left it for after school—after I'd graduated and escaped Baker Street and all that held me there. After I'd discovered a way to take my brothers with me.

But I couldn't quit. Not now. The closeness of Lily's dad's murder had made the crime interesting to me. The photo brought it even closer, made solving it feel like an opportunity to discover another one of Mum's secrets. That it also was an opportunity to get lost in the confusing mire that was Sherlock Holmes? I couldn't let that stop me.

I took a deep breath and grabbed my book for maths, shoving it into the messenger bag at my hip. Then I stood, perplexed, staring at my locker and wondering where my book for maths had escaped to.

Sherlock appeared at my side so suddenly, I half expected a soft puff of smoke to surround him. "Morning," he said, his lips jerking into a grin like a nervous tic. Without warning, he pushed his face too close to mine.

I fell into my locker door to escape him, so that the edges dug into my back. "What are you doing?"

That was apparently not the answer Sherlock expected. I could almost see his mind racing for some possible context. It took only a second or so for him to snap back, "Kissing you."

"You can't just walk up and kiss someone like that." He

was still too close, so I sidestepped to put more space between us and then slammed shut the locker door.

His confusion elongated his face. "But I thought—"

"Thought what?" Admittedly, my tone was angrier than I felt.

Sherlock scowled and turned so that it looked like he would just walk away, but at the last moment he turned back, pointed a finger at me, and said, "You did."

He was right. I had. And in some fool moment, I'd even meant it. But I wasn't about to start up some dumb teen fling. Not now. I had too much else to do.

"It was just a kiss. God, Lock. You're like a kid sometimes."

"A kid," he echoed.

"Like when I hold your hand to calm you down when you get worked up, right? It's what I do with my little brothers."

His eyes went blank, like he just turned off. "And the kiss?"

"I only kissed you because you needed a distraction. And it had been a long day." And because I wanted to. But that wouldn't help, so I kept it to myself.

I watched his coldness return, watched everything about him harden to glass, and wondered if the next thing I said wouldn't be the divot that started a spider's web of cracks. Would I eventually shatter him? I wondered. That'd be a trick. I was the one who felt too fragile to keep talking.

I softened my tone. "I—I just can't now."

He nodded as though I'd said the sky was blue.

I was practically whispering when I said, "You wouldn't like me if you knew me." And I had plans for my life. Plans that didn't include a boy or his junior detective crime-fighting fantasies.

He nodded again and looked to the ceiling when he said, "Boats today. I think I found a pattern."

And then he stormed down the hall away from me, leaving me with my plans. Only, just then, they didn't feel like nearly enough.

Sadie Mae stood in my way in the hall, so that I might have stomped straight into her if she hadn't put her hand on my shoulder at the last minute. "Wow, bad day?" was her only reaction to the seething glare I offered whoever it was that was in my way. She laughed after she said it, of course, in that way she had that always pushed me off my guard.

"Not many good ones this week. You?"

"I'll just say right here that whoever thought up the idea of paying dead white authors by the word should have a special place in hell with the rest of the sadists."

"Literature, then?"

Sadie opened her giant bohemian bag, which she'd probably sewn herself, to show me the tonnage of paperbacks she was hefting around campus with her. I was surprised the stitches weren't giving way. "No idea why I thought I'd want to go to Oxford. I mean, what self-respecting Southern belle chooses to do this to herself?"

"If only you were better at maths."

"Math," she corrected. "This is not a plural word in my culture."

I laughed for the first time that day—perhaps the first time that month, if I were to think back. It was barely a stuttered hiccuping thing, but the sound brightened Sadie's whole expression.

"I don't suppose you'd want to study together, like we did back when?"

That thought was sobering. Sadie used to come to my house and stay deep into the night, sprawled on the floor with one of my pillows and her stack of reading. My house didn't even seem like the same place anymore. I was pretty sure Sadie wouldn't stay long if she did come over now.

"So, that's a no."

"No," I said quickly. "I mean, yes. We could. Just not at my house. Things are . . . different."

I knew we couldn't go to Sadie's dorm. Her dorm mother was the second coming of Stalin when it came to guests. That Sadie managed to regularly sneak in past curfew was a testament to her criminal tendencies.

"Library, maybe?" I offered.

"Say the London Library and I'll be yours forever."

"Sure," I said with a grin. "London Library."

Sadie's expression brightened again and she batted her eyelashes. "You do know the way to my heart."

"I can't tonight. I've got to get out of this thing I said I'd do. But Thursday?"

She prattled off a where and when we'd meet, and I wondered if she'd actually be there when I showed up. All I could do was try.

x x x

By the time Sherlock and I were in the middle of the lake in an orange boat with a light-yellow bottom, I had almost decided it might be easier to duck out of our little game and discover what I could on my own. But the minute he pulled a stack of papers from his messenger bag, all my thoughts of leaving shimmered from my head. Front and center on the very top page was the Man in Green from the photo, one of the three men Mr. Patel stood behind. FRANCISCO TORRES, FOUND DEAD IN PARK, the headline screamed above his head. I snatched the printout from Sherlock's hands and skimmed the article, which pointed to the irony of an infamous bank robber, who'd been released on a technicality after serving only half his sentence, falling victim the very next day to the petty theft of a mugging in Regent's Park.

"What does this have to do with anything?" I managed to choke out. I forced myself to return the article with a smidge of disinterest in my expression, but not before memorizing the date and page number so I could find it later.

"You said Patel was in trouble with the law. So was this one."

"Two isn't a pattern," I said, though my mind was already weaving together too many ways that it could be.

"Correct, which is why . . ." Sherlock slid another printout from the middle of his stack and handed it to me. A smaller headline this time, with a head shot of Mustache Man, who had been tried for some elaborate banking scheme but never convicted. He, too, had been stabbed to death in Regent's

Park, the apparent victim of a robbery gone wrong.

Sherlock's final printout was an obituary for Todd White, sparse on details other than a long list of family who'd survived him and now lived in Lewes, where they ran some kind of herbalist shop. It felt more like an advertisement for the shop than a write-up of his life. The obituary didn't even have a picture, but Sherlock never did anything halfway. Stapled to the printout was what looked like a cabbie license picture of the Striped Man from the photo of my mother. All four of the men standing in a group were dead, as if the killer were using my photo as a check-off list for his victims.

"Three more victims. All petty criminals not paying for their real crimes. All dead of stab wounds. All found in the park."

My eyes roamed around each of the articles as though some secret were hidden in the speckled margins. "How did no one see this before now?"

"You ask this? After the endless incompetence we saw the other night?"

"Not every policeman is like those we saw." Only Blue-Hair Girl and Stepdad were left, and their faces swam through my thoughts as I handed the pages back to Sherlock. "Were there no others? It can't be so rare for there to be stabbings."

"None in Regent's Park. These all happened within the past six months. But I went back three years."

"None in the park in three years? That can't be right."

"Lots in the alleys and streets surrounding the park, and one man beaten pretty badly, but none in the park that I could find in the papers. Of course, if we want to do a thorough search, we'd need access to police records."

"I can get that," I said without thinking. By the time I realized what I'd decided to do, I looked up and Sherlock was smiling. "Why so smug?"

"I thought you might quit our little game. In fact, I was pretty sure you'd do it today."

"And maybe I still will."

Sherlock shook his head. "You're hooked. But never mind that. I'm hooked as well. It's compelling work, this." He leaned back, his elbows resting on the prow of our little boat. His smug smile lingered as he stared out across the lake.

"Truly, Lock, just when I find a way to tolerate you." I attempted a burdened sigh to accompany my words, but Sherlock sat up again, his eyes alight. I thought perhaps he'd come up with another clue.

"'Lock.' You called me that earlier. I like it. Never had a nickname before." He leaned back again, this time crossing his arms behind his head and closing his eyes.

I slid the pages off the seat and read the story of Todd White, ex-con-man turned cabdriver. He'd been off the police radar for fifteen years before he was found dead—stabbed cleanly in the heart, his body sprawled across one of the large planters on a central walkway in Regent's Park. He'd been the first, actually. The second page of the article had a picture of the planter. I'd walked past it a few times in the past six months. I even remember wondering what had happened to the flowers on the one side, never for a moment imagining they'd been crushed under the weight of a dead man or ripped out to remove blood evidence for the police.

The crimes were starting to feel too close. One dead man in a photo with my mother could still have been coincidence. Four dead men felt like it meant something. It suddenly felt imperative to know my mom's part in this group. Were they merely friends at university? Did they work together?

"What do you see?" Lock asked.

"Nothing."

"You've been staring at that page for minutes. It's not nothing."

I didn't really want to admit that I'd just been lost in my own thoughts, so I let myself really study the planter for a few seconds before answering him. It looked like an old fountain with two tiers that had been filled in with soil and then lush plants. It even had a large finial at the top. But I kept coming back to an ornament on the side that I could barely make out in the pixelated reprint of the original photo.

"There's something here on the planter where the first one was found." I held the page up and pointed to where I meant. "Can you see what that is?"

"It's a four-leaf clover," he said, without looking closely at all.

I looked again. "It could be, I suppose."

"No, it is. I went by there earlier today. There's a clover on one side and a tree on the other."

"A tree." I looked from where we floated to the boathouse and wondered how I could convince Lock we needed to get back to shore and over to the planter without telling him why.

"Want to see it?" He'd sat up and had his hands on the oars before I could answer, and sooner than I'd imagined, we were standing in front of the six-month-old crime scene.

I ran my hand over the Celtic knots mixed with leaves that flowed from the branches and down to entwine with the roots at the base. Just like Mom's coin. She was every-where in this game, connected to these people, possibly even to their deaths. I had to know that connection. "They don't really seem to fit the planter's other decorations, do they? The symbols?"

Sherlock walked from our side to the other and then back. "You're right. It's like they've been plastered on, not carved from the original stone." He grabbed an edge and tried to shake it, but the medallion didn't come loose. "Long time ago, maybe."

It had to mean something—this man who'd known my mom, dying at a planter that held the symbols of our secret coin. But I couldn't indulge in those thoughts just then. I couldn't let Lock see me indulging them anyway. What I could do was find out more about Mum—who she really was when she wasn't being our mom.

I knew only one place to do that. And it was more danger-ous than stealing a thousand police files.

Chapter 9

The next two days I came home from school fully intending to make a thorough search of my mother's things, but Dad was always in my way. It was as if he had returned to his old, lingering ways, from before Mum was sick. He went from never home to always home in the space of my decision to invade his and Mum's personal belongings, which almost made me think he'd gained psychic powers. Psychic powers that could only ever come from the bottle, the office, or home. He never went anywhere else. Not since I'd decided to pry, anyway.

Lock and I met in the hall at school and again at drama, in the very back row of the theater. We compared notes and read through the articles I'd committed to memory the very first time he'd handed them to me. We talked details and argued theories, but the longer we went with only the papers as our source, the more frustrated we both became with merely guessing. Lock's frustration, however, seemed to outstrip my own by miles. I was starting to suspect there was more to his mood than just his desire to solve the case of a murder in Regent's Park.

"One of the park regulars then," he proposed, for only the third time in so many days.

"Still a theory."

I watched his grip tighten on the papers in his hands. "What's that supposed to mean?"

"That's what we call it when there's no proof. And there's no more proof of that today than there was the last time you said it."

"We don't have enough data!" He tossed the papers in the seat between us with a carelessness that instantly set me on edge. Nothing I said was adequate that day, even when I was blatantly and obviously right. He was being an idiot, and I might have explained that to him at length, but I was in too foul a mood to be bothered.

Instead, I snapped back, "I said I'd get the file and I will."

He stared at me for a few seconds and then stood and started down the aisle. "Find me when you do."

Getting the chance to go through my mother's things was still top priority, but in the interim, I spent the rest of my spare time trying to find a way to retrieve a bloody police file without my dad finding out about it. I looked through his bag every night after he sloshed into his room to sleep off the drink. I even tried going down to the station, twice, to see if I could talk my way onto a computer or into a file room. With almost fifteen hundred officers in the Westminster Borough, one would think I could slip in and out anonymously, but both times I was forced to hide and sneak out to avoid what few detectives I knew.

Really, I should've just told Lock it was impossible, but every time the subject came up, I managed to lose my head in the challenge of it, in the imperative to find out more about the deaths of my mother's friends, and then I'd renew my promise. As I did that Wednesday out on the lake in the park.

Sherlock was in a particularly awful mood, which I at first attributed to the fact that he was nine full minutes late to the time he'd set (and proceeded to text me reminders of every ten minutes for an hour). It was the first time he hadn't been waiting for me, which wouldn't have mattered at all if he hadn't blurted the word, "Apologies," at me in a tone more suited to insult than regret.

We went out in the boat, but I was quickly aware that his mood hadn't improved in the twenty-four hours we'd been apart—only now I was stuck out in the water with his stormy demeanor. It took exactly thirteen minutes for me to tire of his thunderous barking and heated silences.

"Take me back," I said.

"What are you talking about?"

"You can either row me back to the dock or I will row myself, but I'm done being subject to this mood of yours that obviously has nothing at all to do with me or the file, which I will get when I am able to and not before."

I thought he might take advantage of the opportunity to rid himself of me, or perhaps call my bluff to row myself with another of his pouty silences. Instead, he stood up in the boat. I resisted the urge to grasp the edges as we began to rock. He quickly sat down again with a sigh. I wasn't sure what exactly this little departure had accomplished, but it seemed to loosen his tongue.

"I'm sorry," he said. I started to speak, but he interrupted. "And yes, I know what for."

But he didn't say what for, just stared across the water in the direction of Baker Street, though he couldn't see anything through the fog. Finally, he turned back and rested his hands on the oar handles.

"My mother is ill."

A flare of something painful went off in my chest. Those were the exact words I'd said to Sadie Mae just months before. Hearing them, I felt like the air had been sucked from me, but I still managed to say, "You don't have to say more."

He didn't speak for maybe a full minute, didn't look at me, didn't move—except for his hands. His fingers grasped and released the wooden seat at regular intervals, then reached up to hold the oar handles again.

"She won't go to the doctor." His voice broke at the end of his statement, but he cleared his throat and listed the rest of what he had to say as though he were recounting the facts of our case. "We've tried to convince her, but she won't go, and now she can no longer move from her bed. We don't know what there's left to do—"

"Lock."

"She is the most stubborn woman, and neither of us has ever been good at telling her no—"

"Lock."

"We've tried everything to get her help. She tells us we're

the men of the house but then won't let us do this most important thing—"

"Lock."

When he finally did stop talking long enough to look up at me, I thought perhaps I could see what he must have looked like as a child. A lost child.

His right hand gripped and released the oar handle, and I reached out, covered his hand with mine. I didn't know what to say. Of all people, I probably should have. But nothing anyone said had ever helped me.

He opened his mouth to speak and then shut it and furrowed his brow. He pulled out his cigarettes and stared at my hand covering his a moment, before shaking the box and pulling one free with his lips. He lit it one-handed and blew the smoke out to meld with the fog coming off the lake, all without looking away from our hands.

"I know," I said at last, though I couldn't look at him when I said it. "I mean, I understand . . . how it changes everything."

He cleared his throat and shifted his hand a bit under mine.

"I never asked why you were crying that first night—the night you told me your name." He took a deep drag and blew it out across the lake. His voice lowered. "I never thought you'd tell me if I had."

I withdrew my hand. "You were right."

He nodded and didn't seem like he would ask again. Still, I said, "Six months ago. Cancer. She wasn't even herself anymore for the last three."

"Was there nothing that could be done?" he asked quietly.

"We thought for a little while that there was a treatment, but it was experimental and we didn't have the money. It probably wouldn't have worked anyway." I paused, wondered why I was telling him any of it, before adding, "There's not always something to be done."

Sherlock didn't look at me or register any emotion, really. He just nodded again and threw his cigarette into the lake. "I'm thinking of switching to a pipe," he said.

And that was the end of our sharing. We sat in silence the rest of the time we were out in the boat. An odd silence, really. He didn't fidget once. I didn't feel the need to speak. And even though we never touched each other or made eye contact, even though the lake was fogged in and I had only my cardigan to warm me—I felt comforted. Better, somehow, for the silence than I'd been before it.

I had to wonder if this was what people meant when they said it was "a comfortable silence." I wondered what it meant to feel better sitting silent with a boy than to pour your heart out to a best friend or diary or stranger. Sherlock Holmes surprised me again that day by saying just the right thing about my mom's death—which was to say nothing at all.

Chapter 10

The next day I met Sadie in front of her favorite place in the entire world. The London Library is a members-only institution that boasts decades of high literary tradition, dating back to its opening. Sadie Mae became a member before she'd finished registering for her first set of classes at our school and bought me a membership of my own for my sixteenth birthday. Even at the student rate, I was pretty sure it was a spendy gift.

Sadie Mae couldn't be bothered with menial things like money, which meant she'd always had plenty. Though she'd more than once protested loudly about how much it cost to own even a tiny flat in London, comparing it to the palatial mansion she could own in Georgia for the same price. But a library membership was worth every penny, she assured me.

The minute we stepped through the little glass gate and into the main hall, Sadie breathed in deeply. "I'm home," she whispered, with all the quiet reverence most might reserve for only the holiest of chapels. I was entirely sure she was talking to the books. "Meet me at our spot in twenty?"

It really was like picking up where we'd left off. Sadie had spent our first few visits trying to convince me to read novels—as if I hadn't been forced to read enough of those in school. So this became our tradition, go our separate ways to gather what we needed, then sit together and read or study until they kicked us out. "Better make it thirty. I've actually got a few things to look up in periodicals."

Sadie made a face at my clearly inferior choice. "If I didn't know you meant the science journals, I might get my hopes up." She ran off toward the stairs up to the literature section. At least, that's where I assumed she was going. Sadie managed to find fiction in every building where there were books. Or magazines. Or words. I pulled my hands free of my pockets, then trotted off to start my search.

I spun my mother's coin across the table with one hand while typing in search terms with the other. I should have been studying, of course. The class had almost caught up to where I'd left off in trigonometry a month ago. My mind, however, wandered continually back to the photo, to Mr. Patel's death in the park. Had he even had time to think about his daughter before the short sword paralyzed him?

For all its boasts of subscriptions to 750 periodicals, the London Library didn't supply me with any plain news. They were all very dignified and posh journals of higher learning, which is to say, complete rubbish when it came to gossip. I tried first to do a search of my mother's name, and then her maiden name, but there were only a few hits and none seemed to have anything at all to do with her. I spun the coin once more, only this time toward me, and when it finally landed, the glow of the monitor made the clover stand out from its background.

On a whim, I typed "four-leaf clover" into the search bar and stared at it awhile, knowing it wasn't near enough to get anything other than garden and superstition responses. I didn't really know what I was looking for. So far, I only knew that every man who had been in Mum's photo had died, and they'd all been in trouble for the same thing.

I quickly added the words "coin," "theft," and then "robbery," just in case.

Most of the hits were rubbish, but about halfway down the second page was a link to a journal article on unsolved crimes that contained the words "named for the **clover** seen on a **coin**" and "the **robbery** of four major targets."

I checked my watch while the article loaded, noting my thirty minutes were nearly up, and clicked print, to read it later. I pulled up a new tab and glanced over my shoulder before typing "serial murder" in the search bar. The results were a mix of articles on "How to tell if your child will be a serial killer" and lists of the traits and characteristics known serial murderers exhibit—none from any kind of reliable source. Until I found the U.S. FBI report from some kind of symposium about serial killings.

I was lost in that for a time, skimming through points about psychopathy and motivation, through myths and misunderstandings, through pages and pages of theories all punctuated by the truth that there is no one reason or one pattern of behavior for a serial killer. They all do what they do for their own reasons and in their own way.

"Comforting, that," I said quietly.

The word "ritual" jumped off the page at me, however. Ritual seemed to be the one most common trait. As the paper stated, the ritual was the way most serial killers were identified. They killed with the same weapon or left behind a calling card. Our killer was still a mystery, and we didn't know enough to identify his ritual. Or hers. Perhaps Regent's Park was the ritual.

"Or not," I whispered, sitting taller. Wondering was as useless as my search had been, and I had somewhere to be. I checked the time again and clicked print.

I was almost ten minutes late when I snatched the pages from the printer on my way to the reading room. Sadie was already tucked sideways into one of the leather chairs by the fireplace, a giant book propped up on her knees. I took a moment to figure out an answer for when she asked what I'd been looking into, and she'd inevitably ask, but even after I'd thought of three different lies to tell, I found myself still reluctant to take my leather chair and face her.

So far, she'd mostly acted like our little parting hadn't happened, but I knew she could at any point decide we needed to talk things out—my worst nightmare. As if in the history of humanity anything has ever been truly accomplished by talking.

I folded the pages into my bag and grabbed a wayward book from a table. Then I wandered toward my chair, plopped down, and pretended to be deeply interested in whatever book it was. I couldn't seem to read past the first sentence of the page I'd opened at random.

"Found God, have you?"

I glanced up at the top of the page and held in a reflexive sigh. Of all the books in this blasted place, I'd managed to pick up the least likely I'd ever, ever read: the *Bhagavad Gita*. It wasn't even about God, though I didn't feel the need to correct Sadie. I grunted and shrugged, forcing myself to look at every word of a paragraph farther down the page, though I probably couldn't have repeated any of them had my life depended on it.

After a few moments of silence I traded the Hindu text for my trigonometry book and a pencil, but Sadie never did let me study for too long.

"Did you know there are fifteen miles of books in the London Library?"

"Yes, Sadie."

"Some dating back to the fifteen hundreds?"

She had, of course, used these very facts in an attempt to entice me on my first visit to the place long ago, but I refused to look up and nodded before saying, "Yes, Sadie."

"Over a million books—"

"You should, perhaps, busy yourself reading, or you'll never get through them all."

"Ha. Ha." She paused, just long enough to make me think our little chat was over, and then said, "I would, but they add eight thousand books a year, you see."

I offered her my most weary expression just as she threw

her head back to stare up at the stacks of old leather bindings behind our chairs. It really was a sight to see. I'd bet all the gold in the palace that no one had disturbed any of the books in decades. I had no idea what that section was even supposed to be. Probably the biographies of the forgotten.

Sadie, of course, took a different view. "Heaven, Mori. When I die, this place will be transported right up into the clouds, so I can flit about the stacks for hours on end, reading into eternity."

"You'll run out of books," I mumbled, three lines into a trigonometry problem that had stumped me in class. Now it seemed so obvious.

Sadie gasped. "You take that back, Moriarty. Like you mean it."

"Eternity is a long time."

"You think there'll be no writers in Heaven to make me new books?"

I grinned without taking my eyes off my text. "None of the good ones."

Sadie's laugh tinkled quietly. "Dammit, Mori. Right's right, but you don't have to dash a girl's eternal dreams."

I finally joined in her laughter—a disarming laugh as it turned out, because she didn't wait for me to stop before asking, "Do you forgive me?"

"I have to study."

"Course you do." I managed to almost finish the problem before she said, "But how can you concentrate with all this tension between us?"

I could have concentrated just fine before she mentioned the tension. She stared at me, which made me look away, at the walls, the floors, the staircases and stenciled signs. I'd never bothered to look around before, and now I could only seem to notice the inconsistencies. Perhaps someone more bohemian might have found the arbitrary nature of the decor to be homey. I found it—mismatched.

When I thought about it, Sadie and I were a bit like the London Library, really. Mismatched. Ancient wooden panels covering an entry wall, modern glass surrounding the stair. An ornate wooden banister to one floor, and a sleek, minimalist metal sweeping down to another. The whole building was made from a bunch of old residences, cobbled together in a way that would never have made sense to its original members but felt like home to Sadie.

She and I didn't make sense either. I often found her down-home Americanisms more cloying than charming. We had different interests, different goals, and widely different plans for our lives. Our friendship had more or less been cobbled together in a way that probably didn't make sense, and still, being with her felt . . . familiar. Normal.

Like maybe I could remember what my life was like before. Back when she'd be waiting for me outside the theater, like the time maybe a month before we found out Mum was sick, and instead of groaning when I pulled out my dice to determine our way home, she pulled out two red dice of her own.

"To add spice," she'd said.

"You're ruining my probabilities."

"I believe 'enhance' is the word you're looking for, as in, 'You are enhancin' my probabilities.'"

I'd just stared at her.

"It can't be all that ruined, girl. What, so, one in three becomes one in five? What is that, like twenty percent harder?" I was about to give in to one of my most long-suffering sighs, but she didn't even wait for me to react before she added, "And before you fuss at me, Miss Math Genius Moriarty, just remember our conversation about the difference between being smart and being *crazy* smart."

I'd rolled my dice without comment, though internally I was calculating the actual difference between a 1 in 216 chance and a 1 in 7,776 chance.

It was 3,600 percent harder.

She had decided her dice would represent how many shops we had to stop at on our way home and how many things we had to buy at each shop. This, of course, meant that she immediately rolled double sixes.

"This game is my absolute favorite," she'd said, evidently forgetting every other time, when it was the absolute worst. I negotiated her down to one shop and one food stop, where we would try six things—all puddings as it turned out. I had never in my life tried six puddings at once, but there were a lot of things I'd never done until I'd met Sadie.

I had spent the better part of our day together wondering how in the world we were even friends. But that was the day I'd realized there isn't always a reason why. Sometimes you don't even decide to be friends, it just creeps up on you.

Sometimes there are just these moments you share, when you buy six different headbands at Boots and each wear three on your way to Canteen for a crazy amount of cake and ice cream, moments when you take a train down to Brighton in the middle of the night and barely catch the next train back, or when you buy two bouquets each and see who can hand all her flowers out to people on the street first. When there are enough of those kinds of moments, sometimes you can't imagine not having that person around.

Until she's gone. Until that thing that only ever happens to other people is happening to you and no one is calling to help you escape it. I did escape, though. Even without Sadie around, I escaped into the memories of all that we did together the year before. And in those few times Dad would let me sit with my mother while she was mostly unconscious, I told her about all our crazy adventures. If I'd been gone, my mom might never have known about it. If Sadie had called, if I'd missed that time to sit with Mum at her sickbed and listen to her breathe, I might never have forgiven either of us. Maybe Sadie being around while Mum was sick would have ruined her as a friend for me anyway.

So, with her question still hanging in the balance, I found I could honestly answer, "I was never angry."

"You should've been."

I shook my head. Sadie pulled her chair closer to mine and leaned down in an attempt to pull my attention away from my notebook. Annoying, but effective.

"I should've been there."

"It would've changed nothing." I was surprised at the lack of emotion in my voice.

"You wouldn't have been alone."

"I might have sent you away, regardless."

"You might've tried." Her smile was sad but not forced, and she reached up to drape her hand over my arm—her warm brown skin and my cool white providing yet another mismatch. "I should've fought harder, Mori. And I'm sorry about that, because you deserve a better friend than me."

I shook my head again and tried to go back to my trigonometry, but she attacked me in possibly the most awkward hug that ever was. I forced my arm around her back and endured it. Then spun in my chair, the minute she let go, to stare at my trig work until my eyes cleared enough to see the next problem.

I didn't manage to gather any more information on our case the next day, or the day after that, but our next trip out on the lake was decidedly different. Lock had centered on a new theory that I was pretty sure he only brought up to tease me.

"I'm telling you, it's the police," he said for maybe the fourth time since we'd started our discussion. "Maybe it's one. Maybe more. But everything points to a policeman being the killer."

By "everything," I was pretty sure he meant "every made-up fantasy in my own little brain," so I challenged him. "How exactly do you come to that?"

"Well, the most obvious reason is that all the victims are

criminals who weren't fully punished for their crimes."

"That's more a reason for the people they robbed to be mad than the police."

"Yes, but it's more than that. It's what the police aren't saying."

"Oh, really. And what is it that they aren't saying?"

"Serial killer." He paused for a twitchy little smile, which I valiantly refrained from mocking openly. "They haven't made the connection yet, between all the killings, and it is perhaps the most shockingly apparent pattern that has ever been."

"You don't know what they are or aren't saying. You only know what was and wasn't said that night."

"So, you believe there could have been three strikingly similar murders in Regent's Park, and a fourth one wouldn't be noticed by the very detectives who police the park?"

"Maybe." My mind was reeling with a myriad of reasons why, like their not wanting things to get all mucked up by the media, not that I felt I had to justify myself to him. "This is all just your imaginings. It is possible that other detectives know about the pattern, and the ones at our scene just don't know about it."

"Why wouldn't they know? Why wouldn't all of them be on the lookout?"

I shrugged. "Any number of reasons. To keep it from leaking out to the public. To stop mass panic."

"And in the meantime, he just roams free? Killing at will? No."

"Maybe we're making more of the pattern than is there.

Have you thought of that? Without the police files, we have no way of knowing if these crimes are truly connected. It could be there's no connection at all." Of course, I knew the connection, and a part of me was even tempted to confess it all, tell him about the photo and see what crazed theories he'd come up with once he knew. But the people in this photo were my mother's secret—another secret that bound us together forever, just like her coin. But only if I kept it.

Besides, in my mind the connection of the people in the photo to each other and to my mother made it less likely there was a policeman killing people, not more. The most likely scenario was that one of the people in the picture was killing all the others, and whenever I looked between the two main survivors, my eyes couldn't seem to shift off the blue-haired woman. Something about the way she looked at the camera . . .

"The files are exactly why it must be police at the heart of this. Someone must be doctoring the files, keeping the pattern from being seen. And the only people with access are?"

God, he was being smug. "You are wrong. And really, Lock, if you're going to be wrong so much of the time, you should learn how to take it with an ounce of humor. You'll have plenty of time for condescension when you're right about something."

Sherlock climbed forward in the boat until he sat on the bench facing me, so that our knees tapped with every soft rocking wave of the lake. He stared into my eyes in this rather disarming way, and then he said, "You think you're more clever than me."

It was true, but I supposed I should show him a bit of deference. "I am female. That comes with a few advantages."

"Such as?"

"Understanding and perception, a unique worldview, and the power that comes with being constantly underestimated." I made sure to underscore those last two words by staring unflinchingly back at him.

"So, you believe women are more clever than men, but men cannot see it?"

I shrugged, though our staring match probably detracted from my attempt at casual discussion. "We can be, if we assert ourselves. Unfortunately, many do not. And yes, sadly, men see very little when it comes to women."

"So, you are a feminist?"

"No. Feminists fight for equity, which is an unsatisfactory goal."

He grinned. "You're not satisfied with equity?"

"Why should I be? Men aren't. For all our generations, men have fought for control and power. Why should women be satisfied to be merely equal?"

Sherlock shrugged. "I don't understand the need for power, really. There are more important pursuits."

"Only those who have never felt powerless can afford to think like you."

Sherlock tilted his head and studied my face a moment,

then broke into a giant smile that once again seemed to age him backward. "You are brilliant."

I bit back my own smile and said, "I am right."

"You are brilliant and right, and I think we should . . . that is to say, I should . . ." He studied my face again, and before I could quip about his staring, he swooped forward and kissed me, gently and just long enough to separate this kiss from the quick and playful kiss I'd given him. Almost as an afterthought, his palm came up to cup my cheek just as he pulled away and dropped his hand back to his knee. Then, for what felt like the first time in hours and hours, he looked away, down, up at the sky—anywhere, it seemed, but at me. "I thought perhaps such a moment should be marked," he said quietly.

I was still a little breathless when I replied, "We should, perhaps, mark it again."

He leaned in to kiss me again, but we were both laughing before our lips could touch.

"Can't believe I said that."

"Never mind," he said.

I dared a glance in his direction, and sure enough he was staring at me again. Only this time there was something odd in his gaze. Maybe the look someone gives before walking into the blackest of caves without a torch. "Well, then."

He smiled and didn't wait a moment before returning his hand to my cheek and his lips to mine. Though after just a few quick seconds he released me to stare into my eyes. "And again?" he asked, his voice satisfyingly not quite his own.

I smiled and started to tell him how ridiculous he was and perhaps something else, which I forgot utterly when he kissed me again and again, no longer asking my permission, it seemed. Or perhaps I gave it every time I kissed him back.

Chapter 11

The day after our boat ride, two miracles happened.

First, the boys all filed off to bed on time. I was half convinced they had been replaced by changelings who'd grown weary in their years at the faerie courts. But then Michael belched loudly before I could close their door, sending Seanie into giggle fits, and I knew they were all still human. Well, still my brothers, at any rate.

No sooner had I walked down the stairs than the second miracle materialized in the form of a knock at the front door. Of course, not every miracle comes without a price.

"Door," my dad grunted helpfully from his near-permanent perch at the table in the kitchen.

I tried not to indulge in a sigh before stepping down the final stairs and reaching for the doorknob, little knowing that the mundane act of opening the door would be like stepping back in time a full year to the first night I remember Dad drinking.

He and Mum always had wine with dinner, and, more often than not, their date nights had ended in drunken giggling as they fell through the front door and stumbled across the entry and into their room. But the night we found out my mom was sick and would have to stay in the hospital awhile—that she wouldn't get better, even if she came home—that was the first night Dad brought out the bourbon, sat at the kitchen table, and drank until he forgot himself.

That's how I'd lived with it later, the terror of that first night. I'd told myself and the boys that he wasn't being himself when he slapped Freddie upside his head for spilling milk across the counter. That he didn't mean it when I stepped between them and he yelled until his face was red about how worthless we all were, how he should just kick us out on the street to learn to appreciate what we have, and how we were probably what drove our mother sick. I told the police dispatcher that he'd never been drunk like that before, that he would never hurt us on purpose.

He'd never hurt us before that night. He wasn't a mean dad. He never screamed or did anything that particularly scared me. Honestly, he'd barely paid attention. There wasn't one picture of my dad holding me or playing with me in our family albums. Not even one of him and me together without my mom. He just always seemed indifferent, until the boys were born. But from the moment they brought Freddie home from the hospital, the boys were all that mattered. Our albums are full of pictures of boys-only trips and outings to the carnival. Those few times my dad wasn't lingering around the house were when he was off with the boys in tow for another of their adventures.

His ever-present indifference toward me was perhaps the reason why I'd always assumed the things he said that first time, and every "Memories of You" night since, were the things he'd always secretly thought about me, the reasons why he'd never wanted me around. But none of that explained why he'd hit Freddie, why he'd screamed me into a shivering mess on the floor, why he'd gone after Michael for trying to hide. Not even Seanie had escaped a backhand that night, and still I'd made excuses for Dad.

"He'd never hurt us on purpose," I'd told the dispatcher, which is maybe why, when I dared come out from where I'd hidden the boys away to answer the door, I'd found they'd sent my dad's two closest friends to calm him down and assure us that it would be right as rain in the morning. That we'd see how sorry he was. DS Day and DI Mallory had showed up to our house twice more before I gave up calling—one more time than it should've taken me to learn. They wouldn't even take him from the house, or take us until he could sleep it off. It was before "Memories of You," before I'd learned to hold my infuriating smile and wait to stand between him and the boys. We had no warning, no defense, and Day and Mallory made sure we had no escape.

When I opened the door and the same two officers were on our stoop, that memory dug its claws into my brain. That memory was why it took me a while to realize that they were my second miracle of the night. I would never in a million years expect those two to help anyone, least of all me.

"Heya, Jimmy Junior," DS Day said, barging through the

door. "Where's the monster hiding himself?" He headed off to the kitchen without my answer.

"Mori." DI Mallory nodded his head as he, too, invited himself into the house. He flung down his bag and coat by the bottom step of the staircase, stopped a moment to stare at me oddly, then followed Day into the kitchen, where the junior officer was loudly patting Dad on the back and laughing at his own dumb jokes. I stood in the hall, watching them warily.

"Right, well, Mallory here got this idea that you'd want to come down to pub with us for the first night in months. And I tell him, 'Naw! Moriarty's got better things to do than take a pint with the likes of us.'"

My dad laughed without smiling and downed the rest of his tumbler in one go.

"So, let's have it," Day said. "Who's right? Mallory says you'll never pass up a free drink. I mentioned that, didn't I? First round on whoever loses. And I say you'll keep to your hidey-hole, where the real spirits are. Who's right?"

"The gents ask about you, James," Mallory said. "You should show them you're good for more than putting in your shift."

And that's when the miracle happened. Instead of mumbling them out the door, my dad said, "Yeah. All right. Let's go."

Then he left the house. I stood dumbly by the stairs for probably longer than I should have, almost as though I were waiting for him to come back in the door. But he didn't, and soon I managed to snap myself out of my shock and walk slowly and calmly into my parents' room. My dad's room.

It was his room, though it still smelled like Mum's pungent perfume. I caught a bit of sandalwood from the jar of cologne on the dresser as I walked by, but mostly it smelled like Mom—even down to the undercurrent of urine from when she'd accidentally overturned her commode. Near the end. When she could still stand enough to sit on a commode. He'd spent more than an hour on his knees rescrubbing the carpet after she'd passed. It hadn't worked. Or maybe he'd missed something.

I forced down the wave of emotions that threatened to overtake me and started my search for Mum's box. I'd watched him pack up her things not even three days past her funeral, drunk to oblivion, sobbing like a small child, with "Memories of You" playing over the stereo. I might have stopped him, or asked for a few things of my own, but it was the first night we learned what that song would mean for us.

Freddie got the worst of it again. I hid him away with a sack of frozen peas and sat on the stairs as a sentry, to make sure Dad wasn't going to attack us again while we slept. But instead of the giant monster of fury I'd stared down to get him away from Fred, I watched a lost child crawling around the floor of his room, sobbing out empty threats to no one and everyone. "They did this to you. I know they did it. They won't get away with it. They won't."

I didn't sleep that night, even after Dad crawled to his bed, too drunk to remember to close his door. I just stared at the box in the middle of the floor and wished I had the courage to sneak in and steal it away. Instead, I went in the next day and picked up the few things he'd forgotten to pack. Nothing worth keeping, really. Just all that was left crumpled on the floor.

Maybe it was the remembrance of that night that kept me from taking the box down from where I spotted it in the closet. I stared at the garish pink rose pattern the way I had stared that night and caught myself breathing heavily, like I'd just woken from a nightmare. I looked over my shoulder, like a paranoid freak, then turned back and grabbed the box before I became too worked up.

The inside was a jumble of papers and random objects, none of which seemed all that important—random photos of Mum as a baby, business cards, old insurance and credit cards—like he'd just dumped her pocketbook into the box on top of everything else. There was a broken sand dollar, a handprint mold from Michael when he was five, and, on top of it all, an empty picture frame with a few orange Xs drawn on the glass like one of the boys had gotten to it with a crayon. Two books were tucked along the side, a diet and nutrition guide and an ancient-looking copy of The Alchemist. I also found old gloves, a few disintegrating dried flowers, and a wine-colored scarf with gold threads woven through the sheer.

By the time I reached the bottom of the box, I had a stack of photos next to me and I'd discovered exactly nothing that meant anything. Most of the photos were from her preteen years and then of her after she was married. Like a whole segment of her life went undocumented—or maybe my dad just didn't know where those photos were. Maybe none of us would ever know.

I did my best to put everything away where I'd found it, and just when I'd pushed the box back up into the closet, I heard a door slam. I closed the closet door and ran from the room to the stairs, tripping over something in the dark. I managed to catch myself and freeze in place, listening. The small patter of one of the boys' feet jetted across the hallway upstairs, and I released my breath.

When my heart once again found a normal rhythm, I turned on the hall light and looked around me. I found DI Mallory's bag tipped over, a few files spilled out at my feet. And my two miracles became three. I had no idea why Mallory would leave his bag at the house, and I didn't really care. I just didn't want him to think I'd riffled through his things.

Which is obviously why I riffled through his things.

From the front page or so, two of the files looked to be cases dealing with theft at local galleries, both labeled UNSOLVED. The third stopped me cold. I flipped open the cover and Mr. Patel was staring back at me, smiling widely in that forced portrait kind of way—the same picture I'd seen at his funeral. It was the file. The actual file of Mr. Patel's murder, and it had fallen directly into my lap.

I thought about the look DI Mallory gave me right before he went into the kitchen—right after he set down his bag. Had he been trying to tell me to look in it? But that was ridiculous. In no universe does one of my father's lapdogs leave me a police file to peruse. For what? Was he going to quiz me on it later? Was he looking for my opinions?

I shooed the notion out of my head and, instead, focused on what I had in my hands. The file. And chances were, Mallory wouldn't come back for it tonight—not after a full night of drinking at the pub. I had the file, and I had a window of time. I might have smiled my widest smile of the year as I pulled my mobile from my pocket.

File attained. When?

Sherlock responded almost immediately. *ASAP.*

I looked up the stairs. The boys were asleep. Dad would come home drunk and stumble into bed. No one would even know I was gone. *Fine, but it has to be at your house.*

He sent just a number with his next text—*221.* His house number, I presumed. Which meant that all this time, I was a mere eight doors down from Sherlock Holmes and I'd never known it.

The game was definitely afoot.

Lock's house was a lot larger than mine. Maybe even two of mine put together. The entry led to a large living room on one side and an open kitchen and dinette on the other. The stairs were straight ahead. After leading me toward the kitchen, Lock made a beeline for the electric kettle sitting out on the counter. I stood dumbly in the doorway, watching as he checked under the lid and then plugged it in, pulling down two cups and tossing a tea bag in each.

"Hungry?" he asked, his back still to me.

I followed the stripes of the wallpaper up to an ornate molding and across a metal ceiling to the chain that held the pendant over the dinette. "Not really."

I should've known better than to believe that he really wanted to know. I watched him set our tea mugs on a small wooden tray with a tube of biscuits and then pull a plate of sandwiches wrapped in film from the refrigerator. He must have caught me staring at the crustless triangles when he turned around, because his cheeks went a little pink as he explained, "Mother always has something made up for when guests come over."

I followed him to the dinette, and he waited for me to sit before placing the tray and sitting in the chair closest to mine. "You have a lot of guests?"

"No. We don't."

He sloshed milk into both our cups, and then scowled as he handed me mine. "I suppose I should've asked."

"Do you know anyone who doesn't take milk in their tea?"

"Mycroft."

The mere mention of Lock's brother brought a voice from the doorway of the kitchen. "And who is this?" It was as though he'd just materialized there—tall like Sherlock, but stockier, and with sleepy eyes that seemed to take in every detail of the room and still look like they couldn't be bothered about what they saw. Just then, his eyes were turned on me. I couldn't help but stare back. I wasn't entirely sure he wasn't some shadowy apparition. I hadn't heard the front door open or someone coming down the stairs.

"Mori, this is my brother, Mycroft Holmes."

"Mori? And does she have a last name?"

The way he refused to address me directly put me on edge. "It's none of your business," I said with a flat grin.

True to Holmes form, this answer only seemed to intrigue Mycroft. "Do you know my brother from school? You'll forgive my curiosity, but Sherlock's never brought a girl home before. It's an encouraging sign, to say the least."

"*He's* never brought a girl home either," Sherlock said, biting into a sandwich. He seemed quite pleased with the instant antagonism developing between me and his brother. He would.

"I've never had much use for girls, if I'm being honest. No offense to your gender."

"I'm sure womankind is devastated beyond belief." I gestured to the plate. "Biscuit?"

Lock did a rubbish job of stifling a laugh in a slurp of his tea. But Mycroft wasn't discouraged. He stepped in and snatched a biscuit from the plate, ruffled Sherlock's hair, and said, "I like her."

"As long as Mycroft approves," Sherlock said, stretching out his arm to clink our tea mugs together.

"So relieved," I said, drinking deeply.

Mycroft winked at me in his clueless way, and strode from the kitchen to take the stairs two at a time up to the second floor.

"Did you bring it?" Sherlock was grinning at me when I looked back.

I nodded. "It's in my bag."

We finished our tea in giant gulps, and Sherlock grabbed the open package of biscuits from the table before he led me up the stairs to his room.

I'm not sure what I expected to see behind the door, but what surprised me most was how normal Lock's bedroom was. Freddie could have lived in the room, or even Seanie in a few years. The bed was mussed; there were clothes everywhere and even a few posters on the walls. Everything I'd known of Sherlock Holmes was extraordinary. Here was a strange and vivid reminder that, in the end, he was just a boy from London after all. My feeling of letdown meant it was a reality I needed to face.

I dug in my bag for the file I'd pilfered. "I brought the—"

He interrupted me with a kiss, and I smiled, even as I pushed the file between us and pulled free of him.

"Police file," I said, to remind myself why we were there. I didn't want to meet his eyes, so I looked past his head to the brown walls.

And once again Lock found a way to entrance me. The entire back of his door and the door-shaped wall space next to it was covered in papers, in pushpins, and in bright blue yarn. He'd created a map of our crime, and it was amazing. A neat row of our victims' photos was pinned across the middle, each one with a blue string that led to the site of his death on a map of the park, then to the newspaper clipping of his death, then up to a more random jumble of words and the victims' vocations and schools. I stepped past Lock in a trance, my eyes tracing every path, some from the articles he'd shown me before, some new. Some led nowhere, but most ended at a blank page with the word "police" scrawled across it, followed by a hastily added question mark in a different color, which could only be for my benefit.

"What's all this?" My tone held the hush of the sacred, which might have embarrassed me if I wasn't still so amazed.

I could hear the satisfaction in Lock's reply. "You didn't seem to believe my theory, so I thought I'd show you how I came to it in a different way."

The work and persistence it took to create such a map didn't go unnoticed, but what astonished me most was how close it was to the way I saw things in my mind. It was like a translation from my thought patterns to the real world. It was perfectly and completely me.

I realized I was making a spectacle of myself and forced my gaze away, which was when I saw Lock's room in a new light. There were piles of clothes, as I'd noted before, and strange smells that might have been old plates of food but weren't. Because under the piles were the flasks and tubes of his lab, some permanently burned out on their rounded bottoms, some still full of an unidentifiable sticky residue. He had corked bottles of ash and soil stuffed between falling-over books on his bookcase. A box with various locks on four sides sat on his desk, lock picks piled like jackstraws beside it. Little hints of the extraordinary peeked out from every corner.

When my eyes focused again on Lock, who stood a little awkwardly in the same spot where he'd kissed me, I realized they'd been there all along. He'd been there all along, and I couldn't see him through the mess.

I wanted to tell him everything just then. I wanted him to know about my mom, about her coin, her friends, the photo. I wanted him to know about "Memories of You" and to meet Sean, Fred, and Michael. But more than any of that, I wanted to kiss him and to keep kissing him until one of us ran out of air. So I did.

He surrendered first, leaning back just enough to rest his forehead against mine. Out of breath, he asked, "What about the file?"

"Bugger the file." I grabbed the front of his shirt in my fists and back-stepped toward his bed, pulling him along with me. It took him maybe three full seconds to dead-drop the file to the floor and fall down with me on his crumpled covers.

When I fell asleep, Sherlock was curling a lock of my hair around his finger and explaining some ridiculous theory of his that had to do with surviving a fall into water by shaping his body as he slipped beneath the surface. I felt like I'd slipped beneath the surface as well. I was completely relaxed in his bed and in his arms in a way I shouldn't have been with anyone, much less this boy who talked physics in between kissing me and studying my face, in the lazy, contented way I studied his. My last thought had been something about how much bluer his eyes seemed when they lit up with discovery— and how they darkened when they looked down on me.

I woke up long before the sun rose and realized almost instantly how stupid I'd been. I had to get home before someone realized I was gone, and I didn't even know what time it was. I slipped out from under Lock's arm and used the light from his phone to find mine, the case file, and my handbag. Despite my rush, I stood at his door for two timeouts of my phone's light, memorizing as much of the crime map as I could. Then a third, watching how the shadows tumbled into the hollows of Lock's cheeks as he slept. And when I started to feel an ache within my chest, I left.

The door had barely clicked shut behind me when Mycroft's voice drifted down from the staircase to the third floor.

"He won't know why you left."

I didn't exactly flinch at his words, but it took me too long to respond to what he'd said. Too long again to think of how one responds to a statement like that. "Have you considered wearing a bell around your neck?"

He was sitting on a step near the bottom of the stairs, like he'd been waiting for me to come out. Watching Sherlock's bedroom door like a proper stalker, and yet I was the one who felt like I was creeping about a stranger's house in the night. And he knew it. He was in no rush to answer my question and even took a moment to glance down at the fingernails of his left hand, which I noticed were meticulously manicured. "Once, but I found it clashed with my mysterious nature."

"Your creepy lurker persona? Yes, I'm sure that does well with the ladies."

Mycroft might have visibly shuddered. "As I said, I've given up women."

"For Lent?"

"When I was fourteen and kissed my first boy."

I nodded and stared at him. "That doesn't really make your lurking less creepy."

Mycroft smiled in this almost straight-lipped way that I was pretty sure meant he was about to change the subject. "Don't leave."

"He knows I have brothers to care for. He knows I have my studies."

"And yet he will spend all of the morning deducing the infinite number of reasons why you didn't wake him to say good-bye."

"You don't know what I said to him. And it's none of your business." I thought I heard a faint noise from the floor above.

Mycroft must have heard it too, because his chin rose, despite the fact that he refused to look up. "He is my business." We stared at each other for a few long seconds before he added, "I don't want him broken."

It really was none of his concern. I had no reason at all to explain myself or to even answer his ridiculously dramatic accusation. And still I asked, "How do you know he is the one who will break?"

Mycroft's eyes didn't light up like his brother's, but his expression was tinged with an awe of discovery that seemed familiar, despite his droopy lids. He didn't say anything more, just nodded and turned to run back up the stairs, leaving me to go the opposite direction. Once I reached the street, I found that I'd been clutching my shirt at my chest, like I was trying to hide from what I'd just exposed of myself in the house.

But it was too late. They'd both already seen too much.

Chapter 12

I was at the copy shop within the half hour, xeroxing and scanning the file so I could return it to Mallory's bag before sunrise. I thankfully made it back to the house before Dad was awake, and took it as another miracle when the bag was right where I'd left it. Though, in the light of morning, it became obvious to me that the inspector had more likely left the files for my father than for myself. Since Dad was in all probability barely capable of stumbling to bed when he came home the night before, perhaps the bag's continued presence in our hall was less a miracle than I'd thought.

After the boys were ushered off to their school day, I stood outside my house for a few minutes before making an important decision—I was not going to school. I had never skipped school before. Not even when my mother was dying. The week after she died, my choices were to stay in the house or sit in classes. That is to say, stay in a house filled with nosy neighbors, awkward policemen, and their cooing, tittering wives; or go to classes, where hardly anyone knew or cared my mother was gone, and all I had to tolerate were the crowded halls, monotonous lectures, and an incompetent lab partner.

I didn't need to attend class to keep up my grades, or wouldn't need to if the professors didn't require attendance. But I enjoyed certain trappings of academia—the smell of old books, chemicals, and fresh paint; the facts and figures and symbolism; and most of all, the knowing. Knowing more about the things that mattered than almost everyone in the building.

That was why I willingly walked into the embrace of the most monotonous institution on earth, using little tricks and games to keep me sane while reveling in the parts of school that were tolerable. But that day, holding a copy of the file on Lily's dad's death, with the photo of Mum and Mr. Patel in my pocket, I couldn't do it. Lock's game suddenly felt like one of the most important things I'd ever done.

So, I'd decided I wasn't going to school. But I couldn't stay home, either. I toyed with the idea of going to London Library, or to a pub or café, but something about having a copy of the file in my bag made me feel like everyone was staring at me, waiting to find me out.

In fact, it wasn't until I'd had lunch and was out in the middle of the lake, oars safely tucked inside my boat, that I felt free enough to take the papers out for a good read. Most of the file was boring and useless, testimonies by every officer on scene, all saying the same load of nothing. The forensics were minimal and equally useless, with the exception of a note that there were scratches in the tree bark above Mr. Patel's body that looked like four circles. There was a reference to an evidence number but no actual photograph. Could be worth going back to double-check, but could also be some stupid vandal mark that meant nothing.

The coroner's report was interesting but didn't reveal much we hadn't already guessed. The weapon had been some kind of long knife or short sword that had pierced through the throat and into the spine, incapacitating him, then through the heart, killing him instantly. But the text was odd—like the thought wasn't complete. "Victim's wound is the same shape and angle," and then nothing. Not even a period. It was almost as if the coroner had forgotten to finish his thought midsentence.

Maybe he'd seen the connection to the other murders. Maybe he'd thought the shape and angle were the same, but they didn't match in the end. Maybe a million reasons, and I was inflating the oddity in my mind like Lock would've done. I was suddenly very glad he wasn't there.

That wasn't true. I looked around the lake and felt very alone.

I lay back like he had done and closed my eyes against the brightness of the sun through the clouds. I pictured Sherlock's map, and filled in the details from the file, following the strands of information up to the blank page, willing it to fill in with a face. But my mind kept stalling around useless data. Like the way the coroner's sentence had trailed off without warning. Like how the file had been left splayed on Lock's floor, despite our urgency to see it, all so he and I could kiss and talk about nothing and kiss some more.

I sat up with a start when a few drops of water scattered across my face, and almost collided with a giant goose that had chosen a flight path directly above my boat. I'd drifted up against a bank without realizing, and when I looked out at the lake, the light seemed muted, the shadows different. I'd fallen asleep.

I was late.

And, as happens when one is late, it took most of a year to row back to the café, and apparently everyone in London turned in their boat rentals at four thirty-five in the evening. So, by the time I got through the queue and started home, it was nearly five, and I was sure I'd walk in on World War Brothers or something worse. I never imagined another bad night would come so soon.

I heard the strangled sounds of "Memories of You" when I was still two stoops away from ours and suddenly wished I'd stayed lost in time out on my boat. I didn't start running until I smelled smoke. I was up the stairs in two giant strides and left my keys in the door so that they clinked together like chimes after the door slammed open. No smoke in the house, but I dropped my bag and followed the scent down the hall and past the stairs, where it suddenly overwhelmed me. By that time, a steady trail of papers and photos led me straight to the French door that opened to our tiny patio garden.

There, squished into the only corner that couldn't be viewed by our neighbors on all sides, stood my dad, huddled over our largest stockpot, which was smoking and flaming for some reason. He shoved his hands into the box that held

Mum's mementos and pulled out pages by the fistful to scatter over the flames, then went back for more before I could scream, "Stop it!"

His eyes were red and his cheeks were wet, but his expression was almost animalistic. "Go to your room."

"What are you doing? Why are you burning her things?"

"They're *my* things," he growled back. "My *private* things. And I won't have your filthy fingers touching my things. I'd rather they were gone forever."

"Those aren't yours. They belong to all of us."

"THEY ARE MINE!" He threw the box to the ground, and I watched as it tipped over, spilling the contents across the concrete of the patio. A picture of Mom as a child slid into a small puddle near one of the planters Michael had meticulously cultivated into something beautiful. I wondered briefly if he'd been out watering when Dad had started this mission.

"Everything of hers is *mine*." He squared his shoulders at me, like he did whenever he was ready to start on one of his tirades about my worthlessness. Only this time, I didn't smile. No hand on my hip. I couldn't take my eyes off the photo that was already curling as it waterlogged. I did see him wave his arm wildly toward the mess as he resumed his shouting.

"This is all I have left. I lost a wife, and all I have left is this box of garbage!" He clenched his teeth and ground out his next words. "And you couldn't leave that be. You couldn't even leave me that."

It had been me. I had done this. I'd gone into the box and somehow he'd known it. I'd created tonight's version of the hateful, bitter troll that once was my dad. It occurred to me that I couldn't remember what he was supposed to look like when he was being normal. It had been so long since I'd seen his normal self. Maybe that self no longer existed.

"That's not all we lost," I whispered. Or maybe I said, because he went from stock-still to charging toward me in an instant.

It all happened so fast in that cramped space, and yet slow enough that I saw the change in his eyes. I knew without a doubt that he would hit me for what I'd said, but I still wanted to believe that he wouldn't. I had to believe it. He'd already destroyed so much with how he treated the boys, perhaps a part of me thought his refusal to touch me meant he recognized it was wrong, meant he could still somehow come back. Be different. I was the final line in the sand. The minute he crossed that line, there was no getting him back. So I stood resolute, watching him come at me, and forcing myself not to run.

Maybe we'd never had a chance of his coming back anyway.

I lifted my arms to guard my face, but he pushed me so the back of my head smacked against the brick of the house. I instantly felt wet on my scalp, but I couldn't lift a hand to feel for blood. I couldn't move.

"What did you say?"

I stared into his eyes, barely breathed, wondering if I'd survived the worst of it, if I could stop it, if it were inevitable or avoidable, if I could just work out the right thing to do. The music started to skip while we stood like that, too close for too long, until I felt like I would faint if I didn't take a full breath. And then he turned his back on me and returned to his fire—his destruction of all we had left of her.

I couldn't stand helpless and just let it happen. I couldn't stay quiet.

"I said I lost more than a mother when she died."

He spun on me, and I didn't realize he was going to hit me again until I was leaning back against the bricks of the house and wondering which hurt most from the blow, my cheek or my neck.

"Tell me," he barked. "Tell me what *you've* lost."

I couldn't speak, so he came at me again. I scrambled back, so only the tips of his fingers connected, leaving stinging scratch marks across my already swollen cheek.

"Tell me how much you love her, now that she's gone. Say it. I dare you to pretend you didn't hate her when she were here." His next blow was a backhand to my other cheek. I tasted blood in my mouth, and realizing he'd hit me whether I spoke or not freed my words.

I ran my thumb along the side of my mouth to wipe away whatever it was that dripped from my lip, and blinked away the tears that fell. "I did love her. And you can hit me all you want, but it won't make me think I didn't."

He raised his hand and I flinched away, so his open hand cuffed my ear. I felt sick and dizzy, suddenly wondering if spewing on him would make him hit me harder or leave me alone.

"And I'm glad she's dead," I mumbled out, despite the

screeching alarms in my head that begged me to stop. "I'm glad she died before she saw you turn into this."

He grabbed my hair and pulled back so hard, it felt like my scalp was ripping. He forced me to look at his ugly face. I hated his face. I wanted to shred it with my nails and stomp it from his body. But all I could do was return his raging hate with some of my own. If he was going to kill me, I wasn't going to let him see me afraid to die.

"You're pitiful," I started to say, but his fist slammed into my stomach hard enough to steal my air and send me to my knees. He tossed me away to fall the rest of the way down, and I immediately curled into a ball, expecting his scuffed-up boots to finish me off. I gasped short breaths for longer than I expected—long enough for him to stomp off into the house. But I didn't move until the music was righted. The warbled piano. The sound track for my escape. I crawled my way into a hunched stand and ran from the house, barely taking the time to grab my bag and keys on the way out. Only one thought screamed through my mind over and over.

Never again.

Chapter 13

I sat out on the front steps of Lock's house for what must have been an hour. I didn't know why I was there, but it was dark, and the slats of the metal banister felt cool against the puffy skin of my cheek. I wondered how long I could hide there without being discovered, how long before someone came home or walked out the front door. Perhaps a part of me wanted Lock to find me there, but not so much that I could convince myself to knock.

I shifted my cheek to another slat as my mind riffled through plans of escape for the morning. I could wait until I knew my dad would be gone, pack bags for me and the boys, and then charm the headmaster to get them out of school without Dad's permission. We could be in another town in mere hours, starting over. I could get a job, present myself as their mum, put them in state school. But with no money for an apartment, we'd be living on the street. Too many of us to hide from the police. Too many ways things could go wrong.

Mycroft appeared at the bottom of the stairs like an

apparition, interrupting my thoughts. "When I told you not to leave, I didn't mean . . ."

Too late, I remembered the state of my face. Before he could say something, I tried to hide it again in the shadow of my hood. I'd already seen enough pity from Mycroft.

"Come inside."

I wouldn't have gone in. Had he touched me, blocked my path down the steps, or even brushed by me to hold open the door, I probably would have run off to find a new place to hide. Mycroft didn't even reach to help me up. He waited. When I was ready, I stood, and clutching my arm to my stomach, led the way up the steps to the door.

I felt the heat of the room against the bruises on my face and yanked at my hood, willing it to better protect me from the light in the hall. "Is he home?" My voice was scratchy and monotone, filled with more disinterest than I felt.

"Tea?"

I stared at Mycroft for a few seconds before I nodded. I followed him into the kitchen and slumped into a chair in the nook. He prepared everything in silence, only speaking with his back to me.

He dropped an ice pack covered with a thin, clean dish towel on the table in front of me, and then walked away before asking, "Do I need to call the police?"

I didn't reply at first, but the longer the silence drew out, the more it felt like my nonanswer was somehow affirming his secret guess at what happened. "I just came from the house of a DS."

The kettle got louder as it heated, and Mycroft watched it calmly. "You have brothers?"

"Three."

"All younger than you?"

"Yes."

He nodded and said, "Very well," then poured the water into two mugs, dropped bags into each, and walked out of the kitchen without a word. I held the ice to the back of my head while leaning forward to rest my forehead against the table, and before the tea could oversteep, I heard footsteps on the kitchen floor. Sherlock. He stopped and moved toward the tea before coming toward me.

"Tea?"

I didn't move or speak. Still, he slid the mug in front of me. I heard the chair next to me slide out, but Lock never sat. Instead, he wandered back into the middle of the room and stood so silently, I was forced to peek out to see what he was doing. He was staring at me.

"Show me."

I stared back down at the floral-patterned tile floor, knowing I couldn't hide my face forever, wishing I'd never come inside. When I did finally look up, I turned my right cheek toward him and brought the ice pack to the other side of my face. I knew my dad had hit me there as well, but it didn't feel as swollen. I kept my head tilted down, too, so that between the hood, the dish towel, and my hair, as little of my face would show as possible. My stomach ached, even when I didn't move.

"I need to see if you require medical care."

"I'm fine."

He stepped toward me and stopped again. "Show me. I need to see."

I thought about showing him. I wondered what was running through his mind just then. Was he angry for me? Sorry for me? Merely curious? "Never mind. It doesn't matter."

"It does. You should at least let me—"

"Leave it." I clenched my teeth and took a breath to keep from shouting. "I don't need help."

"You are being stubborn. I merely want—"

"Leave it!" I glared up at him, but my shouting didn't make him step back or flinch. His expression was the same one he made when contemplating how much milk to pour in his tea. "I know what I do and don't need. It's my body, and I say it doesn't matter."

"If you don't need help, why are you here?"

"Great question." I started to stand, but my stomach muscles cramped up, forcing me back down into the chair. I rested my forehead on the table again and waited for the cramping to pass. Lock took yet another step toward me, but I slammed my fist onto the table, and he stopped. "I don't know!" I yelled into my chest. "I don't know why I ever come here. To be studied like a rat? To play this bloody game with your bloody rules that mean nothing to anyone! Or maybe I just love the way you refuse to act like an actual person, even for a moment." I glared up at him again. His face was passive. "More awkward staring? Is that all you will ever have for me?"

He said nothing.

"Is it? I asked you a question, Sherlock. Can you not answer me even a simple question?"

I was being completely unreasonable. I knew I was, which was worse—like being forced to watch someone who is not yourself using your body to be cruel and bitter and ridiculous. Lock only repeated his question in his same stupid, emotionless voice.

"Why are you here?"

"I don't know!" I stood up, staring him down.

I realized then that my face was completely exposed to him. And instead of hiding, I reached up to push back my hood, offering him the full effect of my injuries under the bright kitchen light. He didn't flinch, didn't soften. His face didn't even hint at an expression. He just stared down his beakish nose at me, as though not even my pain could faze him.

But I needed his reaction for some reason. Needed to know I could hurt him. It was ridiculous and petty, and so much more important to me than it should have been. I was willing to do anything to get at him, apparently, because in the next moment I caught myself saying whatever came into my mind, which ended up being nonsense. Or truth.

"I'm here because you're here." I tried to stay angry, to cut that statement with something mean, or at least cheeky. But, instead, I left the words to echo between us.

"Why?"

I shook my head. I had no answers for what I didn't know myself.

"Why me?" he asked. "You must have other friends. Actual people."

Internally, I winced at the way he lobbed my words back at me. Still, I took what I deserved. He was right, in a way. I knew loads of people from school. There was a time when I was never home before curfew, barely checked in on weekends. It felt like a very long time ago, that. I had Sadie and others, in fact, but I hadn't called a single one when my mom got sick. I suddenly wondered what that meant.

I didn't speak for a long while, and every second of the silence felt like a twisting cloth, coiling tighter and tighter, until the very air seemed to pulse like the throbbing in my head. Finally, he spoke.

"I don't matter to you," he said, in his very best fact-listing voice. "That is why you come here. You can do what you like and show me the bad things that might drive someone else away, because it doesn't matter to you if I leave. You wouldn't care were I gone tomorrow. And that is why—"

"You're wrong." I hadn't spoken loud enough to interrupt even his quiet little tirade, but the sound of my voice stopped his. "You are so very wrong."

I felt a wave of emotion well up inside me, and closed my eyes to quash it, to no avail.

"I'm never wrong," he said.

"You are always wrong." I forced my eyes up to his, wondering if there had been, perhaps, a crack in his stoicism from my words. He quickly covered if there had.

"Then—" His brow furrowed before he stared again. "Then answer me why."

"You," I started, as my mind reeled with a hundred things

I wanted to tell him, and a hundred I never would. When I did finally offer an answer, he was standing much closer than I remembered, and that made it harder to speak than it should have. "You have somehow become the first and last place I run to."

"When things are bad," he said.

"Good, bad . . ." My shoulders slumped, and it felt like all my remaining strength whooshed out of me with my next exhale. "I think of you first. I need you to know and hate to tell you. You are the only person I can tell, but . . ."

"But?"

The blank of his expression should have kept me from revealing any more, but there was nothing left within me to stop the words. "I don't want you to know."

Did he soften then? Or did I just wish that he would?

"What don't you want me to know?" His voice betrayed what his eyes didn't—pain. I'd done it. I'd hurt him. And now I wanted only to make it better.

I closed my eyes and felt him move closer, close enough for him to reach a hand up to cradle my swollen cheek. I thought I ought to flinch away, but I was desperate for his touch. I would have leaned into his hand if I weren't afraid of the pain. His thumb gently traced the skin below my eye, and then he leaned in and brushed a kiss just where the ball of my dad's fist had struck hardest. I shivered and he surrounded me, but not all at once. We moved in awkward increments, Lock waiting for me to step into him before his arms pulled me tighter. Then again. And again.

Soon, I was listening to his heartbeat thump against my ear, hiding my eyes in his shirt, and wondering how long I could stay there before one of us would move and ruin everything.

"Come upstairs?" he asked.

"I can't. My brothers."

"Mycroft will see to your brothers tonight."

A ribbon of relief fluttered through me, even before I asked, "How?"

Sherlock shrugged. "He has his way. I'll never understand how he makes things happen; they just always go the way he wants."

We stared at each other for an unreasonable amount of time until I said, "Then, yes."

His thumb traced gently under my eye once more, his next words spilling out more hesitantly. "What . . . don't you want me to know?" I shook my head, looked down, but his hands surrounded my face gently and brought my gaze back up to meet his. "What is it?"

"Me," I said. "I don't want you to know me. Not like this." It sounded stupid, but sometimes truth sounds stupid.

He nodded once. "Then you are the puzzle I will never try to solve."

I didn't believe him, but it didn't matter right then. I took his face in my hands and pulled him close enough so that all I could see was his eyes. I didn't know how to thank him or what to say, so I kissed him like I would never stop. I didn't want to stop. It was the most painful kiss I'd ever had. Also the most perfect.

x x x

I jerked myself awake, then tried to sit up, but my stomach muscles declared revolt until I lay back down. I tried again and managed to prop myself up on an elbow. It's always disorienting to wake up in someone else's bed, even worse because I was pretty sure I wasn't in bed when I fell asleep. In fact, the last thing I remembered was kissing Lock while he tried to make me keep the ice on my face. How that became me under covers—

"I didn't suppose you'd be asleep long. You were a bit fitful." Lock sat in the windowsill, a violin resting between his chin and shoulder. His fingers slid up and down the neck of the instrument, forming practice chords that only he could hear. Instead of a bow, a long, brown cigarette drooped from between the fingers of his other hand. I caught myself following its every movement as he flicked away the ash, pulled it up to his lips. I caught my fingertips brushing my own lips and jerked my hand down onto the bed.

"I'm sorry," I said. But my heart wasn't really in the apology. I was too busy remembering everything that had happened before. The trail of my mother's things. The fire. My dad's fist. Yelling at Lock. Kissing Lock all the way up the stairs. "I didn't mean to fall asleep."

Lock blew a stream of smoke out the window and did a piss-poor job of hiding his small smile as he tossed his cigarette and took up a bow. "There's been another killing in the park," he said before he slid the bow across the strings, taking up his silent song right in the middle as if it had been playing aloud the entire time. "Another man."

I'd never been more grateful for a change of subject. Our eyes met briefly—just long enough for Lock to bow his head in a slight nod—his agreement that we didn't need to talk about my dad anymore. On any other night I might have nodded back or smiled. But I was too fragile to do anything but stare at him while my eyes filled with tears. Another indignity after a long night of them. Luckily, I couldn't see Lock's face. I could pretend that I was imagining the slight strain in his voice as he stopped playing long enough to speak.

"A particularly brutal killing. It appears our killer is losing more of his control."

"Did you observe the scene?"

He played a few overly complex chords and then stopped once more. "I came to get you, but I was told you weren't home. And you weren't at school."

Was told. It was an elegant way of avoiding a reference to my father.

"I had to make a copy of the file," I said. "I skipped school."

He was told.

"What is it?"

By my dad. Because my dad was home, playing that infernal song.

Sherlock's playing obliterated whatever I'd been thinking from my mind, and most likely kept him from hearing my answer.

"Nothing." I dropped my head back to the pillow and tried to ignore the little bruises and cuts I felt. I wasn't ready to wrap my mind around anything associated with Dad. I felt . . . numb. And I needed it.

I rolled over, putting my back to Lock. I didn't want to think about him either.

"Do you think . . . ?" he started. "No. I mean, I don't suppose you could get . . ." I turned back just long enough to watch him shake his head and swing his violin back up under his chin. "Never mind."

"I'll get the crime-scene photos," I said. His walls weren't painted brown. It was wallpaper. A micropattern that made it all look one color from afar. Was it houndstooth?

"We don't need—"

"I'll get them."

Lock's hand was suddenly in mine, but when I glanced back at him over my shoulder, he was pondering the still-open window. His violin had somehow crawled back into its case. "Not worth it," he said quietly. His gaze shifted to our hands. So did mine.

"School in six hours." Lock's thumb stroked the back of my hand and then stopped.

I looked up at him, but he was still staring at our hands. I felt the need to speak but didn't know what to say. I knew what I wanted, just not how to ask. And he was unreadable.

"Do you want more sleep?" he asked.

I shook my head and rolled back over, pulling him down onto the bed with me. For a long time his body was tense against my back, his arm moving every minute or two, like he couldn't find its resting place. I lay still, waiting. And just when I thought he might finally settle down, he launched himself over me, crawled under the covers, and lay facing me, his nose only an inch or two from mine. "I have something to confess."

I swallowed, waited. A thousand worst-case confessions slid through my thoughts, emptying my mind. He didn't say any of them.

"I can't stop thinking of ways to make him pay for hurting you." He slipped his arm around my waist and pulled me closer. "I thought I was more evolved than that. But my obsession with revenge"—he slid his hand up my back—"with wanting to keep you near me from now on, I fear I'm outing myself as the Neanderthal I never thought I'd be."

I leaned in and rested my lips against his for as long as I could, partly to shut him up, partly because he was making me cry again, and I couldn't let him see.

"You should be offended for your entire gender."

I smiled and this time pressed at least ten minikisses to different parts of his lips before he spoke again.

"You really shouldn't reward me in this way. I'll become an insufferable brute."

"You're right," I said with a sigh that blew up my bangs. "I suppose I should leave."

I started to roll away from him, but he caught me and pulled me back into his arms, into his warmth, his smile. We were still playing a game, I thought, until our gazes locked and our smiles fell. The silence made our breathing loud, but louder still was the way he looked at me then. A white noise of a look. Everything else fell away and still I became fully aware of every place his body touched mine, of how my hands splayed across his chest.

But my body held too many memories to be silent for long. My stomach started to ache again and I looked away, remembering what a swollen monster face I had. I could suddenly feel Lock's gaze on my hot, damaged skin, studying my cheeks, maybe deducing what kind of hit would cause each mark. I wanted to squirm away, or at least turn in his arms, but he leaned forward and rested his forehead against my temple so that I could feel his whispered words against my cheek.

"He can't make you less than you are. No one could."

Before he spoke, I might have said there was nothing anyone could say to make anything better. But Sherlock wasn't anyone. He was mine. I felt that in the way his fingers slid down my cheek, in the racing of his heart, and the way his eyes called mine back to his. His lips found mine slowly, warm and soft as he kissed me, then again, and again, until I was breathless and kissing him back.

I wanted to tell him that night all that I'd held back. More than once I parted my lips to explain about the photo, but he kept finding new places to kiss me, washing away anything that wasn't a sigh, a caught breath, a breathless silence. I stared into his eyes, readied myself to tell about the symbols on Mum's coin, on the fountain, but the heat of his hands on the bare skin of my back distracted me from my suspicions. His touches so gentle, always aware of my pain, made me believe it was possible to replace bad with good.

His bare skin against mine, and I could be someone else. Someone he'd still like once he knew what I'd been hiding.

I could be us for as long as I needed and not remember anything at all. I could be lost, and forget, and pretend it would
be right as rain in the morning.

So I did.

Chapter 14

I didn't know how long I'd been staring at Sherlock's string map of the crimes when I finally realized that he was right. Maybe it had been minutes. Maybe hours. It was so easy for me to get lost among the lines. To trace them over and over, even when I knew their outcomes so well, I could've re-created the diagram in all its complexities for myself. But lying in his bed tilted the string world just enough to make me see the whole.

I slipped from under the covers, pulled the closest piece of clothing I could find around me, which happened to be Lock's crisp white uniform shirt, and watched the way the moonlight highlighted some paths and not others. I saw each piece slowly, the dates, the faces, the times, the geography, pins marking the places within the park that had become crime scenes. I watched as they came together into something I could see all at once—the shape the crimes made on the map, the dates the victims died as related to where they stood in the photo I still kept in the pocket of my jeans.

But there was something about the dates. Something familiar when I looked at them as a whole. I saw them in a line, the dates of the crimes. Then saw another line, the dates of my dad's song. I could trace it so perfectly then, Lock's deduction. It had to be a policeman, but probably not for the reasons he thought. It was because of the dates.

September 18. The day of my mother's funeral. The day Todd White died at the planter.

November 23. My mother's birthday. Our first without her. Grant Reeves's—Mustache Man's—last day alive.

February 10. When Mum and Dad met at the tea dance. When Francisco Torres died.

I could hear their song. In my mind, as I recalled the dates and added them to the spaghetti of clues on the wall, I could hear the trembling piano, the bleat of the trumpet. And standing in the dark of Lock's room, far away in time and space from Dad's turntable, I felt my heartbeat speed in my chest.

March 4. Not even my brother's stupid ringtone could drown out the trumpet as it came in. Mr. Patel.

March 26. Stepdad? Blue-Haired Girl? I didn't even know their names yet, didn't know if either one was really dead. But there had been another murder last night. In the park. That meant there was only one left. One person left in the photo. One last chance to know anything at all about my mother and her secrets. Why this was all happening.

Somehow, I'd gotten dressed. Somehow, I'd made my way outside and down the block to where the song should have been playing. But wasn't. Not anymore.

I paused at the front door, my hand trembling as it hovered over the knob.

The boys. I had to check on the boys.

I needed clothes for tomorrow.

Her things. They might still be sprawled out across the patio. Someone needed to rescue them.

I had so many reasons to be there, but the minute I opened the door and found my dad missing from his bed, I headed straight for his closet, where I knew the box would be—returned to its rightful place, though warped with water damage on one side, and ripped along the corner seam.

This time there was no careful method to my search. I riffled through what remained in the box until my finger sliced open on a broken shard of glass. It was still there. I wrapped the sleeve of my shirt around my finger as best I could and kept searching until I had three broken pieces of glass and a metal frame. I pieced the glass together in the frame, then slid the photograph out of my back pocket and smoothed it out on top of the glass, smearing my blood through the shirt across the back.

I didn't care. I was too close.

It took what felt like hours to bend those filthy little metal pieces down to secure the frame backing. But then it was done. I swiped my fingers across my forehead and stared at the back of the frame. At the useless thin metal triangle that made like it would hold the thing up on the wall. At the little easel stand that would hold it up on the table.

I might have stared for minutes before I realized there was a flick of white escaping from under the easel stand—a tiny wisp of a thing, but I pushed my fingernail under the stand to follow it and saw two words written in my mother's perfect script: "Sorte Juntos." I was sure I'd seen those words before, but they didn't seem important enough to distract me from my true task—that thing I was afraid to know, but knew already.

I turned the frame over.

Little orange Xs marked out each face on the photo perfectly. There was even a fifth. He'd marked off his latest victim—Stepdad. That must have been when he'd seen that I hadn't put the things back in the box correctly—why he took everything out to be burned, the reason for his tirade—because he'd gone into the box to mark off the victim from yesterday. That left only one face unmarked, Blue-Haired Girl.

What was it I'd said? That it was like the killer was using my photo as a checklist?

He didn't need mine. I'd thought the park had been our killer's ritual, or maybe the sword, but clearly it was this. He had Mum's copy of the photo, and just like every other serial murderer, he had his own ritual—to come home and mark out the face on the glass. Only, he was smart enough to remove the photo, so that no one would know what the mark was for. Perhaps he'd been carrying it around in his back pocket. Just like me.

Sherlock had been right. The killer was police. The killer was Detective Sergeant Moriarty.

Sitting there on the floor of my mom and dad's room, I closed my eyes and saw everything again. Like the killer stepped out of the shadowy blur he'd been hiding in since that first night in the park. And his face . . . he was my dad. My dad with a knife.

The knife. I thought I'd have to rip apart his room to find the short sword from my mom's aikido kit, but it wasn't even hidden. When I tried to return the box to the closet, this sweater kept getting in the way, so I finally pulled it out, and the sword clattered to the floor, sliding free from its hilt just enough to glint at me in the soft light streaming in from the hall. The house creaked just as a sleeve of the sweater fell free and swayed in front of me. My heart jumped and my face ached as a chill spread through my chest. My hands trembled as I rolled the short sword back into the sweater and shoved it up next to the box as quickly as I could. Then I closed the closet doors and leaned against them until I could breathe again.

I'd left the frame on the floor. The orange crosses seemed to glow on the glass. I half expected the metal of the frame to feel hot when I reached for it. I couldn't seem to pick it up. It felt heavier than before when I finally did. I hid it up my sleeve, for lack of a better place, and walked out into the hall.

Sorte Juntos.

As I crossed the spot where I'd tripped over DI Mallory's briefcase, the words flashed through my mind. They had been typed atop one of the files in his bag. He'd left more than the Patel file to see, and I'd ignored the rest like an idiot. Mallory was clearly starting to put it all together, and now the files were gone and I couldn't find out what he knew.

I took the stairs up to my room slowly, my mind racing

through every possible logical reason why Mallory would bring those files for my dad to see.

I made it up only three steps before I heard footsteps behind me. Running footsteps and then soft puffs of air. I turned quickly, clutching the frame to my chest, but the silhouette in the doorway wasn't the right shape to be my dad.

"What are you doing here?" Lock asked. He stepped into the light as he closed the door behind him, and everything about him being in my hallway, half naked, with his hair sticking up on one side—it all should've shocked me from the thoughts pounding in my head like a heartbeat. But all I could think to do was get upstairs and hide the frame where no one could ever find it.

"The boys," I said, in this weird, quavering voice. "I have to check on my brothers."

"They're not here."

I glanced up the stairs as if I didn't believe him. "Where are they? Seanie will forget to brush his teeth."

Sherlock paused before he answered. "Mycroft said he took them to stay with Mrs. Hudson. He woke me and told me to go after you. That you'd want to know."

I still stared up into the darkness. Only a few steps separated me from my room. "Who is Mrs. Hudson?"

"She was our nanny when my mother still worked and comes to help out now that she's ill." When I said nothing, he added, "She makes sandwiches for tea."

"Sandwiches," I echoed. Like the ones Lock had served me.

"They are safe." Lock crossed from the doorway to the stairs in three steps, and was standing on the step right below mine when he said, "You've got blood on your forehead." He looked me over. "And on my shirt."

"I need fresh clothes." My voice was still this high-pitched wavering thing that didn't sound like me at all.

"Are you hurt? Will you show me?"

He was staring right in my eyes, though he was standing below me. The steps made us exactly the same height. I untangled my injured finger from the shirt and held it up, while still clutching the concealed frame with my other hand. A bead of blood blossomed out until it was so heavy it dripped down my finger as Lock and I watched.

"What happened?"

I shook my head. "I don't remember."

And I didn't, just then. I felt like I was walking in a dream. Only the sharp edges of the metal frame digging into my skin made me realize it was real. I slowly let my arm fall then slide behind my back, counting off seconds in my head to make sure I wasn't being too obvious about it.

Our eyes met again and I realized this was the moment when I could tell him everything. I could show him the photo and the frame and admit all that I'd held back. It was probably my last chance to share it all and have him still forgive me for keeping it secret. My heart sped up at the thought, and I caught myself studying his eyes, like anyone could see anything in a person's eyes. Like they wouldn't just tell me what I wanted to hear. Like somehow the look of his eyes would make me say what I wouldn't. Couldn't.

Perhaps I could have, if only there were more than one of the group left. But he'd waste all his time thinking the Blue-Haired Girl was the killer, and I knew better. I knew she was in danger. But more important, she was my last tie to the version of my mom from the picture. And I had to know her secrets. I couldn't live my life not knowing.

He'd have to understand that someday.

I parted my lips to speak and closed them again. And before I could say anything, I threw my arm around his neck and kissed him. The skin on his back was cold, but everywhere his body pressed against mine was warm. I held him close even after our kiss ended, rubbed my uninjured fingers across his shoulder, as if I could warm him in that way.

"Why did you leave?" he whispered.

"I was coming back." I kissed his temple and reached up to smooth down his hair. "I'll always come back." I don't know why I said it. It was one of those stupid unkeepable promises that are worth nothing. But the words made him grin, so they were at least worth that. "I need fresh clothes."

"We have nowhere to be. Besides, you look good in my shirt."

I smiled. It was too tempting to hide in his room for a day. For two. Forever. I kissed the cold tip of Lock's nose and said again, "I need fresh clothes."

"I'll come with you."

I shook my head. "Stay here, so we have warning if he comes home. I'll just be a minute."

Lock stared after me as I ran up the stairs, and our eyes met just before he turned to face the closed front door as sentry and I turned the corner toward my room. I stopped in the bathroom, avoiding the mirror as I washed my face and then dressed my wound. But I slipped up when I brushed my teeth and came face-to-face with my swollen cheek, my cut and swollen lip, the darkening bruise on my temple that was spreading down to my chin. I didn't even look like myself. Didn't feel like myself either, so maybe it was for the best. I had this sudden feeling that I was on the verge of something—that something big was about to happen. That if I wasn't prepared, it would run me over or pass me by, and I couldn't decide which was worse.

I shook off the thought and escaped across the hall to pack an overnight bag and change out of his ruined shirt. I pulled the shirt tight around me for a few seconds before taking it off. It was cold in my room—a cold that wouldn't go away, even after I'd changed into my own clothes.

Nowhere in my room seemed a safe enough hiding place, but it wasn't like I could carry the frame around. At the last minute I tucked it into my overnight bag and headed out, grabbing an oversize hoodie from a hook by my door for Lock. I froze when I heard the front door slam and practically ran into Sherlock, who was suddenly in the hall. I grabbed him and yanked him into my room, then stood by the door.

I didn't even have to see my dad. It was like my body reacted to his presence without my say-so. My fingernails dug into my palms. My jaw clenched. And I was angry, so angry I was calm. Still. Like a still pool of molten lava, burning from my insides out. I knew if I moved even an inch, it would take me over. If he moved even an inch closer . . .

His bedroom door slammed shut, and the burning broke like a wave, leaving me a trembling mess. I stood at my door listening, counting off the time it might take him to start up that wretched song, but he didn't. The woman in the photo was safe for another day.

I turned, still leaning against the doorjamb, desperate for Lock not to notice my breakdown. He wasn't looking at me. Lock sat on my bed, staring at the program for my mother's memorial, propped between the alarm clock and lamp. He lifted his hand like he was going to touch it, and I said, "I keep it there so—"

"I know why." With his eyes still on the program, he reached up to take my hand. "Of course I know why." I stayed silent, my gaze on him, his on the program, for a long, awkward minute before he asked, "Does it work?"

"What do you mean?"

"Does it keep you from forgetting?"

I ignored the question and pulled my hand free. It was jarring to have him in my room, seeing what no one else could see. But worse was how comfortable I was with him there. Knowing this. Knowing me like this. I glanced around my room, wondering what else of me was on display for his deductions—what else he'd seen already.

The pictures of friends that I'd shoved into the frame of my mirror to make my mom happy. Did he know that I only knew half the names that went with the faces there? Notice that none of the pictures was of me standing with them, except for the pictures of Sadie Mae and me from last year? Did he notice that the only picture of my mother in the room was the one on the front of the program? Did he gain some insight from how tidy I kept the room? From the colors?

I turned back toward Lock, only to find he hadn't seen any of it. He still stared at the program. It occurred to me that perhaps he was wondering how long it would be before he had one of his own. I should have said something reassuring, but all I could think was that I didn't want him to touch it, and we had to get out of the house still, and I wanted to see my brothers, to let them know that I was all right.

"It's probably safe to leave," I blurted before his fingers could brush even the corner of the pristine blue paper.

He nodded and stood, tearing his eyes from the program just long enough to sweep them around my room, saving the image for later, I was sure.

We didn't speak again until we were half a block from the house.

"Maybe we could go and see my brothers. Just so they know I'm okay."

Sherlock paused before he said, "It's the middle of the night."

I glanced up at the sky and furrowed my brow. It wasn't that I hadn't known, exactly. It just hadn't seemed relevant until I thought of a little old lady refusing to answer the door at four a.m.

Sherlock stepped in front of me to stop our walking. "And perhaps you don't want them to see you like this." He traced a finger down the side of my cheek, so that I covered it with my hand. "Give it a day or two for the swelling to go down."

I stepped around him. "Tonight is an anomaly. We cannot stay gone from the house. He can't know we're gone."

"You can't go back," he said firmly, taking my hand, as if he thought I might run back right then if he did not. "It's not safe."

I stopped at his door and spoke quietly. "It's never been safe."

Sherlock took a short pause before following me inside, just long enough for me to hide the way my face crumpled at my words.

Chapter 15

It wasn't true, what I'd told Lock. I didn't sleep any more that night, thinking about what it used to be like in my house—how safe I used to be. I remembered listening as my dad had walked the halls, remembered watching as he looked in on the boys asleep, pretending to sleep when he looked in on me. Or maybe those were someone else's memories too, like grandparents who weren't mine and a blue house with a garden I'd most likely never seen. It seemed impossible for that man to be the man I knew now.

I stared into the darkness, exhausted. I was tired of thinking. I felt like all I'd done in the past few weeks was think and work on this game of Lock's.

That wasn't true either. I'd been lazy, letting Lock run all the errands and do all the searching while I kept all the secrets. The only evidence I'd managed to collect had been a worthless police file. The collective of everything I'd done had only managed to end with me getting tossed around our patio.

All of that had to stop. It was time for me to step up.

Problem was, I didn't know what that meant, exactly.

I could turn my father in, though it didn't take much to deduce the eventualities of that choice. If they believed me, a detective serial killer would go viral, infecting all the screens in England. We'd be celebrities. Labeled. Separated. In the system. And every plan I'd ever made for my life would evaporate.

Worse, and the more probable outcome, they wouldn't believe me. They'd send Mallory and Day back to my door to assure me and shut me up. They'd pat me on the head, make apologies to my father, and leave. I'd be stuck in a house with a killer who knew I knew he did it, and my chances of living through that . . .

Don't turn him in? I knew he had only one more target. I also knew he was deteriorating. If he couldn't find her? If her death wasn't enough to quell whatever it was that made him take a sword into Regent's Park . . .

That thought actually made me sit up. I was vaguely aware of Lock stirring in his sleep, of our copy of the police file starting to splay toward the edge of the bed. Because I didn't know why my dad was doing all this. I didn't know what made him hate these people so much, turn so completely against everything he'd ever been.

Maybe they were criminals. Maybe he was stopping them the only way he could. Perhaps that was why the DI left his file so conveniently for Dad, to aid him in his quest to take out dangerous killers. Or maybe Mallory *had* left it for me to find, to stop him.

I sighed aloud. Perhaps wishful thinking was the first sign of madness, and I was on a Wonderland trajectory.

I really had only one plausible choice. I had to investigate on my own. I had to find the woman from the photo, find out what she knew, and make her tell me. But all I had was a photo, and no idea how to use that picture to find her. Untrue again. I had a photo, a living witness out there somewhere, and I had two words. "Sorte Juntos."

Lock stirred again and reminded me of an additional complication. Sherlock Holmes. He wasn't about to give up on our little game, nor would he fail to notice if I were to suddenly be off on my own. I stared down at him for a few minutes, smoothed his hair with my fingers. He smiled in his sleep and turned toward me, tossed his arm across my lap. I caught the file just before it waterfalled to the floor and set it on the nightstand. He smiled again and I felt that tug inside me, the desire to tell him and bring him with me to find my answers.

But I couldn't. Not yet. I couldn't see the end of this path, couldn't let Lock get caught between me and a killer, and until I could protect us better, I had to walk it alone.

I slid down into Lock's arms and stared at the slanted shadows of the pins in his door. "Alone for now," I whispered into the dark.

Sherlock slept on my bedroom floor for two days after the incident. I knew why he was there, of course, and that it had little to do with me. I knew because I understood more than most that life is fragile. Because loving someone means pretending that you can keep them safe when they're with you, that they will be okay when they aren't. You have to believe this to the point of denial, because to not believe leaves you with nothing but panic. A person can't live with that kind of panic. Not for long.

When you lose someone close, when you can't stop the pain or make it better, when you can't even talk to her for fear you'll crack into a million pieces on the floor, when you can't do anything but sit and watch her deteriorate—that's when you realize you can't pretend anymore. All that precious denial disintegrates in a moment, and you're left with the truth.

That life is fragile.

That letting yourself love people is a most sadistic form of self-torture.

That the fully alone are the lucky bastards who never have to learn to live with worry.

Lock couldn't stop what was happening to his mother— no more than I could stop what had happened to mine. But me? He could still pretend to keep me safe. And I couldn't take the last dying tendrils of his denial away from him. So I didn't fight his constant presence, despite the way it infringed on my new commitment to investigation. I couldn't let him stop me from my own pursuits, however, not even that first day. It meant missing school, which had somehow become the very least of my worries.

As soon as Sherlock kissed me good-bye and headed into the swarm of students going to class, I backed out the front door planning to hop the first bus to Regent's Park. I was determined to get a look at the symbol that had been carved into the tree at the Patel site. It might be nothing, as I'd originally thought, but I needed to have all the facts of these crimes if I was going to figure out why my father had become a killer and how to stop him from killing the Blue-Haired Girl. I needed to know everything.

That included getting a better look at the fountain planter where Todd White had died. I pocketed my mom's coin that morning so I could compare the symbols from the coin to the plaques affixed there and look for any inconsistencies. I barely made it out the door, however, when I heard a familiar lilting voice.

"My, my, my," Sadie said, walking up from behind me. "Just six short months and here you are kissing boys and ditching class. Who knew all this time it was my influence keeping you from walking the delinquent path?"

I could probably have invented at least twenty solid ways to disentangle myself from Sadie, but I knew all of them were useless. It would have been a better use of my brainpower to figure out how to answer her next inevitable questions.

"Who is he? And how did you two . . . ?" She lifted her brow and turned back to look at the door, as if she could still see Lock walking the halls. "Not that I don't approve, mind you. He's got a geeky-hot thing going on."

"That is Sherlock Holmes," I said. My gaze had followed Sadie's, only instead of Sherlock, I saw my chemistry professor making her way toward the doors. "And the rest can wait." I grabbed her arm and pulled her down the steps and toward the bus stop.

"Where to, my corrupting friend? I can miss exactly one class."

"Regent's Park."

Sadie scowled. "You make a lousy delinquent."

"You don't have to come along."

"Obviously, I do, or this will be the worst ditching ever."

Sadie tossed a barrage of inconsequential questions into my lap as the bus took us toward the park. I was certain they were leading up to what she really wanted to ask me.

Yes, I supposed we were dating. No, he was not my boyfriend. No, I had not ingested any of his basement experiments that might possibly have been a love potion. No, I did not believe in love potions. The park was where we met. No, I would not take her to the exact spot so she could check it for our "love vibe." And, finally, yes, he was a decent enough kisser, and no, I would not tell her every detail of every kiss.

My smile only faltered on her final question. "I don't suppose you'll be telling me what has happened to your face?"

I had opened my mouth to answer before realizing what she'd asked, then promptly closed it. When she hadn't asked first thing, I'd been sure my makeup had done its job. I should've known it wouldn't mask the swelling.

"Didn't think so."

She never pressed the hard questions. Maybe because I rarely answered them. This time I almost did, but then the bus pulled up to the Regent's Park stop, and I said only, "It wasn't Sherlock."

She nodded, unsatisfied, but seemed ready to leave it there

for now. I made immediately for the park entrance, with Sadie trailing behind. It hadn't occurred to me, until we were actually entering the park, that somewhere in the confines, the latest crime scene was probably still marked off—that there was a slim possibility there might even be something left to see. But I was at the park to find a different clue.

I started a direct route to the Patel scene, but one of the picnic tables that flanked the main path was covered in delinquents. That's what my father would've called them. Mum would've corrected him, said they were just bored and maybe a little misguided, that they could use the guiding hand of a proper police officer. Then my parents would've exchanged a look that I, to this day, do not understand.

I watched a couple of older women in their matching velour walking suits pass by the boys. One of them cupped his hands around his mouth and cried out, "Munters!"

The boy sitting on the table was flicking open a switchblade and then folding it shut over and over again. He was the only one who didn't snicker at the insult. The ladies acted like they didn't hear it. But I knew they did. The one in pink pulled at her jacket, like she could make it cover more of her, and the other stood up taller as she sucked her stomach in.

A boy in a bright orange jersey waved a dismissive hand in their direction. "Park's full of 'em today. Not even a passable among 'em."

Which was unfortunately when they turned their attention our way. We were still a ways off when a boy with a cap pulled low over his eyes nudged the one with the switchblade and pointed in our direction.

"Jackie spoke too soon. Lookie there."

Jackie, who was apparently the one in the orange, stepped forward just as I looked away at the trees. "That one there's passable, but her friend here's perfectly fuckable."

The boys all laughed and one of them hooted. I really didn't know or care which way I'd been classified. I was determined not to show any kind of response, and even tempered my expression and the speed of my walking to prove it.

"Come on, luv! Don't be shy. I got a big one for ya!" The one in the cap grabbed his crotch as we walked by, which I also ignored, though I couldn't see how far behind me Sadie was.

"Oy! I'm talking to you, slag! Cold bitch."

"Shut your hole!" Sadie shouted back, which was when I turned and noticed she was trembling.

Switchblade boy pressed the button on his knife, which snicked open. "Fuckable number one's a Yank! Always wanted to ride a Yank. Wanna come for a ride, babe?"

Sadie turned back toward me, like we were supposed to ignore them and walk on, but the look on her face stopped me cold. I felt that burning in the pit of my stomach I hadn't felt all day—hadn't felt since my father . . . It propelled me toward them. I couldn't stop the smile that formed either, or the heat of the glare I gave the switchblade boy. He must have noticed it too, because he folded the blade shut and set it down next to him on the table.

"Apologize," I said.

"You want some too, bitch? Cuz I've got plenty to go around."

I slowly stepped closer, heel to toe, smile still in place, and when I got so close I could have rested my hands on his still splayed knees, I affected the sultriest voice I could. "You're asking what I want now? I want you to apologize to my friend for being a crude, small-minded, pathetic little asshole who can't keep his moron mouth shut. That's what I want."

I flashed him a smile as he fought to cover his scowl with an apathetic grin of his own.

"I like it when they're lippy," Switchblade said, too loud for how close we were, and then gave me the most predatory look I'd ever seen on a boy. "Like to imagine just what those lips could do for me."

I leaned closer, despite the fact that he smelled of chip grease, smoke, and sweat. I rested my hands on the table to either side of him, then smiled.

He leaned back and said, "What you playing at?" all quiet like, so his mates wouldn't hear, I slid my hand over his knife and then leaned back just enough to slide it between us, unnoticed.

"You still haven't apologized." Now I was the one speaking loud enough for his friends.

"For what? It's a compliment, see. You bitches just don't know when to say thank you." One of his friends snickered, and Sadie stepped closer to me.

"Mori, it's okay. Let's just go."

"You will apologize to my friend now. And then I expect an apology for having to stand so close to your foul stench for the last minute and a half."

He adjusted his jacket and smirked. "Yeah? And why would I do what you say?"

I let my smile drop, let the rage consume me just long enough to cram the top of the switchblade hilt into his crotch. "Because my finger's on the button and I'm not a patient girl."

"Psycho bitch!" He tried to push me off him by my shoulders and scramble away, but I fisted his T-shirt in my hand and shook my head.

"Better not. I'd hate for my thumb to slip. By accident." I narrowed my eyes and whispered, "Wouldn't want to give me a reason to hurt you."

"Sorry," he whispered, and the sound sent a thrill through me. When I didn't move, his voice became this whining, blubbering thing that made my smile true. "Sorry, I said sorry."

"Not to me. To her." I glanced over my shoulder. "And say it loud enough for your mates to hear."

"I'm sorry, miss," he said to Sadie.

I was almost breathless from the pleasure of his submission. It was like a soothing cool had washed over all the rage that had consumed me, making me invincible. I almost giggled when I said, "For what? I didn't hear that part."

"For what I said, okay? It was disre—disrepes—"

"I believe the word you're looking for is 'disrespectful.'"

"I'm sorry, right? I said it, like you told me."

I stared him down for about ten more seconds before

backing away. The minute I turned, he said, "Give it back."

I spun in place and flicked the knife open, which made them all flinch and gave me another surge of adrenaline. Sadie called my name, and I started to laugh. "I think I'll keep it." I spun it around in my hand, blade still open. "It suits me, don't you think?"

This time I waited for the pack to run off before I turned away. Sadie studied me with big eyes until I'd clicked shut the knife and pocketed it.

"That's illegal," she said quietly.

"I know."

I started walking, and she didn't speak again until we were just outside the copse of trees where Patel's body had been found. I must have stopped walking when I saw it, because Sadie said, "Something a cop's daughter would definitely know—the legality of weapons in England. If only we had one of them around."

"If only." I grinned and walked into the trees, which of course all looked the same. So I backtracked a little until I was standing in front of the large shrub Sherlock and I had hidden behind and tried to orient myself.

"Maybe next time you decide to go all superhero on me, a little warning ahead of time?" When I didn't answer, she stood in front of me. "Mori, seriously. You were like a different person just now."

Sadie's plan to get my attention backfired, but only because she was standing almost exactly where the evidence tech had been dusting the umbrella that night. With that context, the whole scene appeared before me again, like it was that night all over.

"Never mind that, we're here." I walked forward until I was standing in front of Patel's tree. I could even make out a stain in the dark soil and tree roots at its base. I resisted the urge to reach up and run my fingers along the gouge that the short sword had made when it had pierced through him. But it was obvious we'd been right. He'd definitely been stabbed at throat height first.

"Here is where you bring me? To a tree?"

"For starters," I said, stepping around to the far side and searching the bark for the etching that was mentioned in the police file. It really was clear as day when I found it—a four-leaf clover. This hadn't been a random meeting place. Patel had met my father here on purpose. The clover was a marker, but I didn't know for what. I didn't know why.

"You do understand what ditching school is for, don't you, Mori?"

I was about to answer when I heard her cry out softly. I turned just in time to catch her hands with mine and keep her from falling.

"Are you all right?"

Sadie started laughing. "Nice catch." Her foot was stuck in a square hole in the ground. "Should've been looking where I was going."

It hadn't been there before, or at least hadn't been noted on the crime-scene report. And perhaps it wouldn't have been. Though it definitely had proximity to where the man died and was almost a perfect square. It was pretty obvious that a person had dug something up. As I looked from the dug-up space to the clover etching, an idea sparked.

"What is it?" Sadie asked.

I apparently wasn't being very subtle in my expressions. "I was just thinking how odd it was that there would be a dug-up spot like this in the middle of the trees." It was partially true, though I was careful to be stealthier as I backed up to the tree and paced off the distance between the etching and the spot. Six paces. Six feet exactly. I had no idea what that meant, but I knew for certain I had to get a look around the newest crime scene. Somehow, and without Sadie or whoever else was around figuring out why.

"Come on," I said, walking quickly away from the trees.

Sadie started laughing, but she followed me anyway. "What are you up to, Mori? Is this some kind of strange treasure hunt?"

I grinned at her over my shoulder. "Maybe."

"What's the prize for winning? And I do mean besides the pleasure of a walk through the park with little ol' you."

"Do they make such a lavish prize?"

We both laughed and she skipped to catch me up, looping her arm through mine. The plan had been to make straight for the fountain from the site, but when we got about halfway there, a big loop of yellow tape appeared just off the main path. Too close to the main path, actually. There weren't even any trees to shelter the crime from prying eyes. What was it Sherlock had said?

It appears our killer is losing more of his control.

I suddenly wondered how well my father had hidden his crimes; if DI Mallory's sudden interest in spending nights out with Dad at the pub had anything to do with his interest in the investigation; if, perhaps, he would eventually be able to put this thing together on his own. My dad could rot in a prison cell for the rest of his life for all I cared, but I wasn't ready for the fallout. I wasn't ready for my and my brothers' lives to change forever.

If my dad was going to be caught, it would be on my terms—when I had a plan in place to protect the boys and me from what came next. And that day was not today.

She narrowed her eyes. "What in the world are you doing?"

I composed my expression into my best smile. "How would you like to help me find my next clue?"

"For the treasure hunt?"

"Sure. But it's inside that circle there."

"That crime-scene circle?"

"Technically, yes. But it's got to be an old one or there'd be more people, right?" It was a blatant lie, which made me the worst friend in history. But I needed her to believe me, just for a little while.

Sadie's forehead crinkled when she raised her brows. "This sounds deliciously delinquent of you." She gave me a devious smile. "I'm in."

Relief and guilt flooded me equally as I turned away from her. The taped-off area was guarded rather loosely by two uniformed bobbies and a plain-clothed, youngish man, who couldn't possibly be more than a detective constable. They were chatting with their backs to us, but one of the uniforms turned before we got too close.

"What happened here?" Sadie asked.

"Some small, boring thing, I'm sure," I answered.

"Yes, because they always bring out the yellow tape for the small, boring crimes."

"All you need to do is distract the police so I can look around."

"And when do I get to find out what exactly it is you're looking for?"

"One day. Two days tops."

Sadie pointed a finger at me. "Twenty-four hours, or I'm out."

I grinned. "Fine."

"Fine," she echoed, and pranced off toward the officers, leaving me to my task.

I took in the whole scene at once, which was pretty much just a grassy area that looked like it hadn't been mowed in a while. I couldn't see too much of where the body had been, other than what looked like a stain but could have been anything from where I stood.

I heard Sadie distracting them brilliantly. "Now what is that funny word y'all use for your policemen?"

As quickly as I could, I sidestepped until I was parallel with what must have been Dad's escape path. The grass was longer on this side and seemed to have been disturbed in only one section—by only one set of feet. I slipped my arm just under the tape, took one last look around, and ducked inside the circle, staying low and following his path back closer to the scene. I knelt down at the edge of the tallest of the grass and took in what I could.

The stain was large and circular and surrounded by grass. Nothing more. It was clear where the police had trodden the rest to bits. But there wasn't a marker in sight—nothing to connect this area to Mom's coin, like the scene I'd just left, like the planter. Nothing to etch a clover into, no dug-up earth like at the Patel scene.

I backed up and ran in a crouch back outside the tape. I barely had time to right myself and pull my hair down over my still-swollen cheek before Sadie warned me someone was coming my way.

"Detective?" Sadie called. "Where are you going?"

The plain-clothed cop offered me a rather sheepish grin and half jogged his way over to where I stood, trampling my father's path to nothing before he reached me. "Detective Constable, actually," he confided to me. "Not that I'll be correcting that Yank."

"Oh, well." I tried to act embarrassed, but I literally cooed, I was trying so hard to cover my groan at yet another incompetence. I should've been pleased. He was exactly the type of copper I needed. "I'm sure it's just that you have such an air of authority about you."

The officer preened predictably and said, "How can I help you, miss?"

"Well." I pointed inside the tape. "Can you tell me what all this is about?"

It took my constable about half a second to decide I was trustworthy before he stepped closer to me and lowered his voice to a conspiratorial level, "Murder, miss. Pretty bloody, actually. Looks like a chap was minding his business along the path in the park and got gutted for his troubles."

I made what I hoped was an appropriate expression. "Sounds gruesome." I tilted my head down to make sure my cheek was hidden in my hair. I was pretty sure Sadie had only seen through my makeup because she knew my face so well, but I was equally sure that a look of pity from this constable would send me back into a rage.

"Yes, well, it comes with the job for me. What brings you to a crime scene at the park this morning? You're a bit late to see anything that matters. The detectives have mostly been through here already."

"I always check out crime scenes," I lied, realizing only after he gave me his first suspicious glance that I'd said the exact wrong thing. I could no longer pretend to be the casual observer I'd wanted him to believe I was.

"Interested in crime, are ya?"

"My dad's police," I said quickly to cover, then internally released the most heinous string of profanity I was capable of forming.

"Oh, really? Tell us who."

I said the name through clenched teeth. "DS Moriarty."

His expression lit up in recognition and my heart sank.

"You're Jimmy's daughter, then? Junior, they call you."

I forced a smile. "The same."

"Aren't you supposed to be at your studies?"

"Free period."

He seemed to take the lie in stride. "Strange, your dad not being assigned this case. He usually works with Mallory on all his cases."

I should have just nodded. Or shrugged. Or have done anything but speak, as it turned out. Instead, I said, "That's my fault. I was sick yesterday, and he spent the whole day taking care of me." As soon as the words left my mouth, I realized I'd never be able to take them back. I'd just made myself Dad's alibi for the time of the crime. I briefly wondered how soon I'd regret that.

"You've got yourself a good one there." His smile was true, but mine was not. He didn't seem to notice either way. "Well, best get back to school before your free period's over, yes?"

I nodded. "Yes, sir, detective."

He preened a bit again and watched as I made my way back to the path and down toward the park's entrance. We were only barely out of sight when Sadie caught up to me. "Mission accomplished?"

"It might have gone too well," I lied.

After barely a minute of silence, Sadie began her prattling on about what class she was missing (composition) and why she wasn't worried about missing it (she'd turned in her essay early), as I led her down a path that veered toward the fountain planter. I hadn't noticed that I'd been walking Mum's coin along the outside of my fingers until a boy walking his dog said, "Cool trick," as he passed me by.

I grinned and pocketed the coin and wondered how long I had until Sadie asked about it. But she didn't. She just kept on about how Dickens's characters were "forced to swim for their lives in the deep dark swamp of his bloviating prose," while my mind carefully traced all the contingencies of what I'd done. How, if the DC mentioned he'd seen me, as he was sure to do, my dad might react to me being in the park at a crime scene in the middle of the day. What Mallory might think. It was stupid to tell the DC my real name and sloppy to be caught hanging around the scene. I couldn't afford to be either.

I almost walked past the fountain planter, once we reached it, but at the last minute pulled Sadie to a stop at the side with the elaborate tree plate attached.

Sadie immediately saw what I had, just days before. "What a weird little planter this is. It doesn't even match. Is this part of your hunt?"

I stepped back out of Sadie's periphery and pulled out Mum's coin. Holding it up to the fountain made it obvious that someone had used the coin to craft the plaque. The tree on the plaque and on the coin were almost an exact match. That had to mean something. I slid the coin through my fingers, on purpose this time, and tried to figure out what. "This might be the biggest clue yet."

Sadie wandered to the other side and said, "Huh. Reminds me of a clock tower in Rome."

"You finally made it to Italy," I mumbled.

"Georgia," she corrected. "Rome, Georgia. There's this big clock tower there that started its life as a water tower. The clock was only added a year after its construction, but it kind of sits on top in this odd way that lets you know it wasn't part of the original. Kind of like these plaques, yes?"

"Yes," I said, catching the glint of the tumbling coin in my periphery.

"Don't lose it," my mom had warned one day when I showed her my trick.

"Is it worth money?" I'd asked.

She'd smiled. "This coin is worth more than money. It's a token. It means you belong."

"To what?"

"To me, and to where I belong."

That had sounded like a riddle to me, so I narrowed my eyes. "Where do you belong?"

I remembered that she looked around our house then. If I'd been older, maybe I'd have known what her look meant, because she didn't answer, except to say, "When you're where you belong, it's like magic. That and a turn of luck, and you'll find your way through anything at all."

"It's like magic," I whispered. My fingers drifted over the plaque, tracing the branches up to the top. It looked even more out of place in the rare bright sun. I splayed my hand across the design, so that each of my fingers slid along a branch, and for no real reason, I pushed against it.

The top half of the plaque tilted forward. I thought at first it was a trick of my mind, or I'd imagined it, because when I pulled my hand back, and pushed at the top, it didn't budge. But with my whole hand on the tree, I was able to tip the plate forward until it clicked. After the click, when I removed my hand, the plate stayed tilted, but I could hear the soft clicks of a timer, as it ever so slowly righted itself.

"What's that noise?" Sadie said, coming around full circle to where I stood.

"It's like magic," I said splaying my fingers to tip the plate again.

"Oh!" Sadie's wide eyes were the brightest amber. "What do you think it does?"

I shrugged. "You try it, and I'll run around to the other plaque. See if it moves or something."

At the four-leaf-clover plate, I tried to tip it as well, but it didn't budge. And then the clicking timer stopped and I scowled.

"Anything?" Sadie called.

I looked around to make sure we weren't being watched. "Try again," I called. Then whispered, "When you're where you belong," as Sadie tipped the tree plaque, "it's like magic." I grasped the four-leaf-clover plate. "That, and a turn of luck."

I twisted to the left. Sure enough, it rotated and slid back, revealing a small compartment beneath. I held my breath as I leaned down to look and found a bunch of papers inside. I glanced around again, my breathing coming faster. I pulled the papers free, and the plaque slid closed, leaving me holding a picture and two envelopes. I heard some footsteps behind me, and turned my back to the planter right as the globular woman who carried all her bags through the park strolled by. She stared hard at the ground, not even acknowledging my presence, but her steps were slow, and I didn't want to look at what I'd taken from the compartment until I was alone. So, I stuffed everything into my bag and called, "Nothing!" to Sadie.

She ran around and pulled and pushed at the four-leaf-clover plaque, but it didn't budge for her. She scowled. "It should spin in circles at least. I mean, if it's not gonna reveal buried treasure or some kind of Victorian animatronic wonder."

"Fresh out of automatons, London is."

Sadie shook her head. "Now what foreign atrocity will I tell my mama about on our Sunday call?"

"I heard something about a swamp of prose today."

She smiled. "A deep dark swamp. And here I thought you never did listen to me."

I tried to act shocked and hurt, but Sadie glanced at her watch and gasped for real. "Late!" she cried, and then ran a few steps backward on the path before stopping to ask, "You coming?"

I looked back at the planter, searching for an excuse. "You go first. I have one more thing to check out."

Sadie grinned. "Delinquent."

I returned her smile. "Teacher's pet."

She winked and took off running for the bus stop, calling back. "Twenty-four hours, Moriarty, and I'll be coming for some answers about all this."

I waited a good two minutes after she was out of sight before daring to pull the papers from my bag. I sat on the next bench I saw and spread them across the weathered wooden slats. The picture was of some old church. On the back was written an address in Sussex, Piddinghoe Village, which sounded like someplace no one ever goes. Down at the bottom in microprint were the two words that I'd practically been hit over the head with lately, "Sorte Juntos."

"Scorpio" was scrawled across the first envelope, and inside was what had to be a fake ID. My mother's younger, smiling face was glued to it, but her name was Ginny Wilkes, and it showed her wrong birthday—a birthday, I noted, that would make her a Scorpio. The second envelope was filled with cash. I didn't pull it out to count it properly, but I thumbed through more than £200 before closing it up again.

It didn't take me long to work out what I'd found. It was her getaway. Everything but the picture fit. My mother had stowed away cash and a new identity in case she ever needed to escape. Which led me to wonder, from what did she need to escape?

Chapter 16

I wandered around the park so long, I didn't make it back to school until everyone was going to their final afternoon class. I started for the library, determined to do a quick search for "Sorte Juntos," but the warning bell let me know I was too late. I rushed into drama just as the final bell rang and sank into one of the theater seats toward the back. I took a deep breath and closed my eyes as the cast filed onto the stage.

Before I could open them again, Lock's voice intruded from the darkness behind me. "You didn't go to class, Miss Moriarty." He jumped over the back of the row of seats and plopped into the one next to me. "You've been skiving off, and now you're caught."

I tried my best to smile at him. "By you?"

"Yes, by me."

"And how do you know this, Mr. Holmes?" I leaned close. "Where's your proof?"

"I sat outside your chemistry class and you never came out." He was awfully cute when he was smug. Irritating, but cute.

"How do you know I didn't just leave class early?"

So, it was more on the irritating side when he leaned in and smelled my hair. "You've been in the park!"

"You can *smell* the park on me?"

"No, your hair tells me you took a bus. Your shoes tell me you were at the park, most likely after ten forty-five this morning."

I looked down, and there were grass stains along the white part of my trainers and little bits of grass stuck to the canvas. "Or maybe out on the football field."

"No, unfortunately for you, our school's grounds staff mows the field after seven each night. The sprinklers come on at dawn, washing those pesky leavings into the thatch. But the park—"

"You are now going to tell me that you know the grounds schedule for Regent's Park?"

He reached down and pulled a leaf off the bottom of my shoe and held it up. "This says you were down at the canal."

I very much failed to restrain my grin.

"You were at the crime scene. Without me."

Lock was also cute when he scowled.

"It had nothing to do with the case," I lied. But then I didn't know what to say next. So we sat in silence for a bit. Lily Patel was back at school, I noticed. I probably should've noticed before then, but I'd had quite a bit to keep track of. John Watson sat cross-legged, leaning against the far stage wall and watching her play her part, an open script in his lap. When she saw him looking, she turned away quickly and walked from the stage.

I slid my fingers along Sherlock's and then pushed them down between. "I'll most likely be gone tomorrow, too. I have to go down to Sussex."

"What's in Sussex?"

"I don't know yet." A truth, and then the lie, "But it really has nothing to do with our case."

Lock didn't say anything, leaving a nice gorge of silence for me to throw myself into. As one does.

"You want to g——?"

"Yes," he interrupted.

I sighed, partly at my own idiocy, partly at his. At any rate, I removed my hand from his. "I will need to go off by myself once we're there."

"I'll be busy taking clippings anyway."

"Clippings?"

"Of the different vegetation to be found down there."

"You want to study the vegetation of Sussex."

"It's on my list."

"Plants. Plants are on your list."

"The regional botany of England and Wales. How else will I know where you've run off to? I don't suppose we'll be going to Wales on the weekend?"

.I rolled my eyes, and Sherlock grinned and steepled his fingers together as he fell into his thoughts.

I retouched my makeup before dinner that night, to keep the worst of my bruises from my brothers, though I didn't for a minute believe it fooled them. I hadn't seen much of my father since I'd caught him out on the patio. He hadn't done as much as look in my direction when we were in the same room, which was for the best, as I couldn't keep my eyes off him when he was near. I also couldn't seem to control my rage enough to keep it off my face. After watching Dad stuff three bites of potato into his mouth and practically swallow without chewing, all I could think was how disgusting he was and how I couldn't believe my mother could stand to be near him all those years. And while I watched Dad, Michael had been watching me. He reached his hand under the table to hold mine, distracting me enough to look away. Unfortunately, my rage-filled gaze fell on Freddie, who shrank back before I could offer an apologetic look.

Dad grunted something and left the table before the rest of us, which made me think I was free of him for the evening, but after everything was cleaned up and put away, I walked into the hall and found him leaning against the banister, flask in hand. It was enough to make me decide to sleep in the park that night.

I made a face and tried to rush past him up the stairs, but he reached out and grabbed my arm. I shook him off and glared. "Don't."

He shifted his weight and stared at the wood of the banister, like it was why he was there in the first place. "You were in the park today."

I silently cursed the entire lineage of that DC.

"Yes or no?"

"Yes." I practically yelled the word, which made Dad look

at me before he remembered himself. With his gaze firmly fixated on the front door, he said, "You said I was with you."

I nodded, not that he could see.

"Why would you do that?" When I didn't answer, he barked, "Why?!"

I shrugged, tried to regulate my breathing and force a calm, but that didn't seem to make my tone any lighter. "Well, he was asking questions that were none of his business, wasn't he?"

Dad finally managed a longish glance in my direction. "Yeah, well." He rubbed the back of his neck and took a drink from his flask. "You'll say the same again if someone asks." He punctuated this order with a single nod, then stomped to his bedroom and slammed the door.

I looked at my arm where he had grabbed it, brushed my fingers over the skin as if I could clean him off me. That his DNA was part of my makeup made me want to retch until I was purged of him altogether.

True to form, Lock had found his way into my bedroom again, still not ready to leave me in this place without a sentry. He seemed to know my thoughts the very moment I stepped into my room. Or maybe it was always his plan to jump up from my bed and surround me with his arms. In any case, he whispered in my ear, "Make an excuse, any excuse, and let me take you from here."

He knew I couldn't, knew why. I'd said it too many times to say it again, and still he responded to my excuse. "We'll bring them with us. Eat Mrs. Hudson's sandwiches and watch movies on Mycroft's tablet until they're all asleep."

I smiled and turned my face into the soft cotton of his T-shirt. "And when he unleashes all the Queen's men to find us?"

Lock shrugged. "We are our own army, you and I. None can stand before us."

After I'd clicked out my light, and before I'd given up on sleeping alone and crawled from my bed to curl up with Lock on the floor, I grabbed my phone off the nightstand and quickly typed "Sorte Juntos" into Google Translate. The words were Portuguese, meaning "lucky together," almost meaningless—or might have been on another night.

For the first time since I'd asked him, I felt glad that Lock would be with me in Sussex. I wasn't sure what I'd find there, but I knew somehow Lock would make it seem manageable—or at least survivable.

I spent most of the night thinking of all the reasons why leaving for a whole day was a truly horrific idea, but there was no way around it. The travel time alone was almost six hours round-trip. I only justified it by reminding myself that the boys would be in school most of the day, and Dad at work, but there were too many contingencies—too many ways this ended badly—for me to let it go. By midnight, I was in the bathroom texting Sadie and asking for her promise to check in on the boys after school, just in case Lock and I didn't make it home on time. She was, predictably, still up reading, and texted right back assuring me she'd even bring over a snack, as she'd been baking again—her way of dealing with homesickness.

Calls home are a special form of torture, she typed. *I miss my family too much.*

About today, I sent back, but then I didn't know what to say.

After a few seconds my phone vibrated. *Me too,* she typed. *We need more days like today.*

I slept fitfully and gave up at four a.m. to sneak down the stairs. Only one more thing for me to deal with—my father's short sword. If we had the time, I would've waited for him to go to work, but we had to be out of the house before any of them woke up or risk having to explain why I wasn't in uniform, why I was leaving earlier than usual, and any assortment of questions that might come with every tick away from my normal schedule.

Dad was snoring so loudly, the stairs were vibrating with the noise. The soft sound of his door clicking open didn't even break his rhythm. A bottle of bourbon with maybe a tablespoon of liquid left was tipped over on his nightstand, a visual clue to the mystery of his deep, deep slumber. I was able to slide the closet open a few inches at a time until I could reach for the sword, where it was still wrapped in a sweater next to my mother's tattered box of things. I had it in my hand and was out the door of his room in seconds, his snores droning on while I rewrapped it in a towel.

The number of people in the park that early shocked me. I should've known it'd be popular with runners and dog walkers, but I'd never come face-to-face with the crowds until that morning. I made my way directly to the bandstand and then toward the lake, slipping inside the curtain of willow branches at the water's edge. There weren't any people there—no one on the water. But still I waited until even the few lingering shadows in the area seemed to have moved away. Removing the sword from the towel was the worst part.

I spent a good five minutes wiping down every surface and scratching the fibers of the towel into every crevice, and then I checked again for early morning park people. I thought I saw a shadow by a tree around the bend from me, but then it didn't move, and I knew it had to be my imagination. Even if it wasn't, it was too far away to see me, much less understand what I was about to do.

After one last swipe of the towel, I threw the sword as far out into the lake as I could without leaving the cover of the branches. It sank immediately, without even a trail of bubbles to show where it had gone in. And then it was done. My father was disarmed, of a sort. Not that he wasn't a trained policeman, capable of killing in a myriad of ways, and I didn't know whether he even knew how to find the Blue-Haired Girl or not, but the sword was part of his ritual, and perhaps its absence would be enough to at least give me a day. So with that chore done and the boys looked after with the promise of American baked goods, there was nothing to do but collect Lock and head for the station.

Even though the train to Brighton didn't leave until 8:37, it was still before seven when I left the house again, this time dragging an eerily quiet, barely coherent Sherlock behind me. Once I got him some coffee, he perked up, but he wasn't very talkative as we took our bus to the London Victoria line. I thought we should buy all-day passes, just in case we needed to turn around quickly or stay late. But when I asked Lock about it, he merely mumbled his assent. Finally, when we were standing on the platform, waiting for our train, I decided enough was enough.

"What?" was his only response to nearly a full minute under my direct scrutiny.

"You're quiet today."

"Thinking."

"About?"

He studied my face before he answered. "How difficult it can sometimes be to keep a promise."

"And which promise it that?"

Another unreasonably long pause. "I once promised a girl that she was the one mystery I would never solve."

I stared across the gap and up to the tiny panes of windows near the ceiling. "That doesn't seem all that difficult."

"I agree. It shouldn't be. And yet . . ."

Someone jostled me closer to Sherlock, and I turned, moving into him without lifting my eyes. "It could be . . . ," I started, but my throat suddenly felt unbearably dry, and my words wouldn't come.

Lock leaned his face down toward mine so he could speak softly in my ear. "I have made an observation of a different sort."

"And that is?"

He shifted his weight from one foot to the other, and his cheek pressed gently to mine. "When a person cares for another, he wants to know everything about her all at once."

I grinned. "Where's the fun in that?"

I kissed his cheek and he kissed mine back, and just when I had hold of his lapels and was leaning up so that our lips brushed, the train pulled into the station, bringing with it a gust of wind that blew my hair around our faces. "I'm sure she will tell you everything just as soon as she is able," I said against his lips. I didn't think he heard me over the noise of the train, but something changed in his eyes.

His lips moved slowly against mine, playfully, teasing a kiss that never quite landed. The platform was a frenzy of movement and noise all around us, and I could only see him, only feel his gentle exhale against my lips. And then he kissed me, but it was the way he held me that made me feel the change in him. His arms completely surrounded me, pulling me in tight. One hand pushed up into my hair to hold me close even after his lips pulled free of mine. He rested his forehead to my temple and kissed my cheek before releasing me slowly—like he didn't want to, like he might pull me back in at any second.

Lock seemed more his old self once we found our seats on the train. He pointed across me to a woman seated on the aisle just two seats ahead of us reading a book. "She is a hairdresser. Tell me when you see it."

I might have assumed the same, just from the elaborate dye job and the critical mass of product that held the curls in her hair in a perfectly natural wave that most likely wouldn't move in a hurricane. But then she lifted her hands to examine her nails, and I saw calluses on her thumb and forefinger. There were tiny hair fragments on her pant legs below the knee, and probably most telling, she was shod in the ugliest, most comfortable-looking Mary Janes of all time.

"Shoes," I said, because I knew it would be the one thing he wouldn't notice. By his immediate glance toward them, I was right. "No one who spends that much time on her hair wears such soulless shoes unless she's on her feet all day."

He didn't comment, but I watched the corners of his mouth twitch before he gestured behind us with his head. "The gentleman behind us teaches chemistry."

"Chalky, cracked fingers? Too easy."

I watched as his gaze flitted from person to person in our car, sizing up and dismissing each in turn until finally he pointed at a girl who was crying in the back corner of our train car. "So, tell me about that one if you crave a challenge."

"What's so challenging about a girl crying on a train? It could be anything."

"Exactly. Girls cry over everything." He obviously didn't see my expression or he'd have stopped talking. "She could've broken a nail for all we know. . . . Or perhaps it is something serious," he added, only after he glanced at me.

I made sure to enunciate when I spoke. "You are an idiot."

"And a Neanderthal. But you'll have to take the blame for that. I warned you what would happen if you rewarded me."

I tried very hard not to smile, but my mind betrayed me by replaying the moments around his warning over and over, until it was inevitable. "Damn."

"Given up so soon?" He went back to studying our crying girl, his steepled fingers tapping against his lips. I joined in, never expecting to almost instantly discover her secret—a secret I was sure Lock wouldn't have deduced were I to lay out the clues before him and wait until the end of time for him to see it.

I quietly cleared my throat and turned to look out at the passing landscape.

"You have given up," he accused.

"I haven't."

"You don't know the answer already."

"Tell me when you see it," I said, still staring out the window. Though I could see his brow furrow in my periphery.

He tried valiantly, my Lock, but he never did note the pale hue of her face, the way her bra appeared two sizes too small, or even the way her hand kept resting across her stomach just before a fresh wave of tears fell from her eyes. I never told him either. When he got twitchy and frustrated, I did give him a hint.

"She hasn't broken a nail," I whispered.

Chapter 17

The first thing I noticed when we stepped out of Brighton station was the smell. Even blocks from the beach, I could smell the ocean and hear the gulls. It was tempting to stay and ignore the chore of travel to a tiny village like Piddinghoe, especially after we realized we'd missed the bus to Newhaven by minutes, which meant another train ride northeast to Lewes, followed by a bus back south to Piddinghoe, and then a walk into the village. I tried to get Lock to stay in Brighton, which seemed the most obvious place to waste a few hours, but he followed me back onto the train, mumbling something about the loneliness of beach towns.

I spent most of our trip talking up the glory of Lewes, not that I knew much about the place. Still, I was able to distract him from following me on to Piddinghoe with a carrot in the form of an Herb Walk flyer that promised a tour around the Railway Land Local Nature Reserve with an herbalist.

"Come with me." His eyes were bright with all the possibilities, though they immediately shadowed a bit when I shook my head.

"I've an errand to run. I'll call your mobile when I'm back."

"Back from where?" He was barely restraining his smile over my slipup.

"When I'm *done*."

"But that's not what you said. You said when you're back, which means you're leaving Lewes."

I stepped close enough to kiss his cheek but didn't. "You promised."

"An impossible promise." He kissed me quickly, then again, just because he could. We stood in an awkward silence for a few moments like imbeciles before finally turning our respective directions. I didn't look back, but his footsteps faltered once, so he could have. I decided to believe he did.

The bus dropped me off on a narrow road in the middle of nowhere—at least, that's what it looked like. On one side of the road, I could barely make out a pond through a chain fence lined with skinny trees. Tall grass flanked the other side, along with a mishmash of wooden fence panels in a variety of colors and patterns. It must have been Piddinghoe, unless the bus driver was a liar. It was definitely the countryside. I remembered the bus driving past a turnoff just before stopping and managed to walk the right way toward it on my first go. The cross street would take me almost the entire way to the address, if Google Maps was to be trusted in such a remote place.

I made my final turn onto a narrow, bendy road that had no placard to name it, and an odd feeling pricked up my neck.

Not so much déjà vu as familiarity—not that I'd walked this road before, but rather that I should remember it. The closer I came to the address, the more intense the feeling became, until I found myself picturing how the road might have been different sometime in its past—a space that might have once been filled with a shack, a giant tree that might once have been thinner.

Walking around the final bend of the narrow road was almost surreal. I saw a blue house first, and immediately felt like I'd drifted back into the earliest of my memories, heedless of the fact that this couldn't possibly be the home of my imagined grandparents. I must have continued to walk forward, because soon I was standing at the top of a gentle hill of bright-green garden plants, poking up from rich, black earth. Flashes of ripe red strawberries and deep purple aubergines peeked out from between leaves, beckoning me to toddle between the plantings on that tiny path, to skirt the bees flying around bright-orange squash blossoms, and to look for ladybugs in the shady places.

It was real, my memory. Which meant I had been there before.

I could almost see a blurred vision of my mother, her arms crossing her chest as she watched me play, her head turning as a woman with bright blond hair emerged from the house—a woman who punched through the vision and continued on a path right for me.

"This is private property," she shouted. Still lost in memory, I needed a fraction of a second to realize she was talking to me, even when she followed up her greeting with, "Who are you?"

She had an American accent, which I didn't expect, and she was older than the blue-haired girl in the photo, older than the blonde in my memory, but still the same person. Her bright blond hair had been replaced with a shiny black that changed her coloring a bit, but it was definitely her. The woman from the photo was standing in real life in front of me, and I could say nothing.

Her eyes went squinty and I thought she might charge up the hill toward me, but she managed only one step before turning back to stare at the blue house, like something tethered her to it. "Who are you? What do you want?"

It was awkward, to carry on a conversation from so far away, but I finally managed to speak up. "I think I was here when I was small."

"That's impossible. My family's owned this farm for generations."

I nodded and stepped down the hill, slowly, like I was afraid the whole place might disappear if I got too close. Before I'd halved the distance between us, the woman's expression changed completely, and she ran up toward me, until we were barely a step apart.

"It's impossible." Her hand came up like she would touch me, and I flinched. She looked past me toward the road and then out across the fields, for a reason I was pretty sure I could deduce.

"I'm alone."

"How are you here? How did you get here?"

"You know who I am?"

The woman smiled the same smile from the photo and raised her hands again. I forced myself to stay still as one hand rested on my shoulder and the other smoothed over my hair. "Anyone who knew her would know who you are. I can't believe . . ."

She grabbed me into a hug, which I tolerated as best I could, and when she finally released me, I managed to step back without being too obvious. "What is your name?"

She laughed. "I've never been good at English manners. I'm Alice. Alice Stokes."

"Alice," I echoed. "I need to ask you questions."

Alice's smile dropped. "Does *he* know you're here?"

I knew whom she meant, but still I asked, "He?"

"Moriarty," she said, like there was something bitter in her mouth. Though she offered me an apologetic grin just after, perhaps realizing she'd spoken my surname too. And my mother's. Thinking of my mother while standing near this woman made me want to climb inside her brain and search for all the answers only she could provide. I suddenly found I had to know everything. Now. I couldn't seem to wait even another second to know.

"I have questions," I blurted.

She stared at me just long enough to make me think maybe the makeup wasn't covering all my fading bruises and then turned to walk toward the house. "Come inside," she called over her shoulder. "We'll talk."

Alice led me to a French door that took us directly into the kitchen. Despite her self-proclaimed lack of English manners, she went immediately for the kettle when we walked through the door, which probably meant she'd lived in England quite a while. Before the water boiled, she managed to scrape together a board of cheese and grapes, some fresh strawberries and cherry tomatoes that looked more the size of golf balls than cherries. I picked one up and smelled it.

"You really do remember this place? You couldn't have been more than three."

"I remember a man and a woman. White hair."

Alice nodded and brought over our mugs. Mine had milk, I noticed. Hers did not.

"My parents."

"I always wished they were my grandparents. Mine are a little awful."

"God, you talk like her and everything. I still can't believe you're here."

I felt a tearing in my chest and furrowed my brow at the sensation. I'd been told of my resemblance to Mum all my life. I half thought it might be the reason why it took Dad so long to come round to hitting me. But this woman said it differently. She made me wish so much that Mum were here sitting with us. I wished it in a way I'd not dared to in six months. I looked down at the scuffed-up table to hide the way my eyes glazed over for a few seconds, then reached in my back pocket and tossed the picture on the table between us to give my voice time to recover as well.

Alice's eyes went wide and she smoothed the photo flat against the table. "Where in the world did you get this?"

"I saw it at a memorial."

Alice grinned. "And you took it? It really is amazing how like her you are."

"Are you saying my mother was a thief?"

"Whose memorial?" she asked, as if my question had never been voiced.

I paused, just long enough to study her face when I answered. "Louis Patel."

She tried to cover her surprise, unsuccessfully.

"His daughter goes to school with me."

"Louis Patel is dead?"

They're all dead. You're next. That's what I wanted to tell her, but something stopped me. Instead, I said, "Sorte Juntos."

Her expression changed again. She was studying me now. "Well, it seems you already have answers."

"Not enough. What does it mean?"

"It's Portuguese."

"I know *that*. 'Lucky together.' What did it mean to—to her?"

"To us." Alice turned the photo back around so that it faced me, then pointed to the man in the green shirt. "That's Francisco Torres. He's the one who gave us the name, and—"

"He's dead."

Alice frowned. "How?"

"A sword," I said slowly. "In Regent's Park."

"And Patel?"

"A sword. In Regent's Park."

Fear in her eyes then, and I wondered if I'd messed up. "Both?"

I stared at her, tried to read deeper into her expression, but all I could see was the fear. "No more answers from me. I have to know about my mother. I have to know everything."

"No. Not everything. No one should ever know everything about her parents."

"I *need* to know."

Alice shook her head, her fingers slowly pushing the photo back toward me. I picked it up and turned it toward her.

I pointed to Mr. Patel. "Dead." To Francisco Torres. "Dead." To each face in turn, and after each face I said, "Dead." My finger hovered over my mother's face, and then I looked up into Alice's eyes and exhaled before I said, "Dead."

She barely breathed. Her expression went blank as what I was telling her sank in.

"They are all dead but you, and you are next. I have to know why. It's the only way I can protect you."

"You know who is doing this?"

I tried not to react as I ignored her question. "I have to know everything."

I sat back to let her process what I'd said, afraid to push any harder, afraid perhaps I hadn't pushed hard enough. It took her maybe five minutes to decide to tell me, but I knew she would three minutes in, when she traced my mother's hair with her finger. It didn't lessen the wait, but it kept me from speaking.

"I loved your mother," she said. "We were babies when we met. Younger than you, even. Fourteen, I think. And from the first moment I met her, I knew she would change me. I counted on it. I was just this American stranger, country bumpkin, lost in the city. Your mom knew London like it was her play yard. At fourteen, she'd already managed to charm every street vendor in a ten-block radius."

I instantly had hundreds of questions but bit them all back to let her tell her story. I couldn't risk that she'd change her mind and go silent again.

"I followed her everywhere, through school, through university. I even stood by her side when she married *him*." Again with the sour face.

"You never liked him?"

Alice shook her head. "I never understood it. He was just some cop. And it wasn't like she was the cop's-wife type."

"And what type is that?"

She refilled our mugs with tea and leaned back in her chair. "Not your mom's type."

For some reason, Alice's answer made me try to picture my dad out in her garden, but I couldn't see it. He didn't fit here among the safety and peace of this place. Though it occurred to me just then that if he knew about the farm, perhaps it wasn't the safe place I imagined it to be. I tried desperately to keep the emotion from my voice as I asked, "Has my father ever been here?"

Alice shook her head. "No. Your mom used to bring you here when things would go sideways at home. And they were always going sideways. Those two fought harder and louder than any couple I'd ever seen. There were times I was sure it would come to blows."

I must have reacted to that, because her expression was suddenly pained and she seemed to be scrutinizing my face. I tipped my head so that my hair hid the cheek that had gotten the worst of it.

"It never did," Alice said. "Or, at least, she never told me."

I shook my head and couldn't look at her when I said, "He never hit her."

She drank half her tea and sighed. "Well, when Freddie was born, a lot of things changed. I saw her less. Once Michael came along, she stopped coming to the farm, and since I couldn't even seem to visit without causing some kind of argument between your mom and him, I stopped coming around." She stirred the dregs of her tea with the sugar spoon and sat quietly for a long time. "I went back to America for a few years." More silence. "I don't know." The pain on Alice's face caused a stabbing sensation in my chest that I couldn't explain. It was like a deep sadness radiated off her in pulses. "I don't know much that's happened since then."

I waited a few long moments for her expression to dull before saying, "That's not everything."

She stood up and walked our mugs to the sink, then stared out the window. "Like I said . . ." She drifted off with her words, into her mind, where my answers were still locked away.

"And I said that I can't help you if I don't know it all."

"I promised your mom. I can't tell until you're older."

I checked my tone before asking, "How old must I be?"

"Older than now."

"And what if something happens to you?"

She turned back to me, still clutching our mugs to her chest. "There's a letter. It's supposed to go out to all of us automatically when something happens to one of us."

"But you are the only one left!"

Alice scowled and dropped the mugs to the counter by the sink with a thud. "You said."

"Where are your letters?"

She slumped back into her chair, her face scrunched up like she didn't want to talk about it. But she didn't seem to understand the importance of my question. "I haven't been home in a few weeks."

"Mr. Torres died six months ago."

"That's impossible."

"You keep saying that, but obviously it's not. They have all been killed but you and my mother, and you haven't received any letters."

Her eyes shifted left to right as she stared at the table, like she was reading words written there, and then she looked up at me. "You know who is doing this. You know who it is."

I sat very still, trying to decide how to answer that accusation. My thoughts teemed with all the reasons I shouldn't say—should never, ever tell anyone what I knew. But I had to keep her safe, and she couldn't be safe if she couldn't see it coming. She was my last connection—the last person who knew my mother before.

I nodded.

"But you don't know why. That's why you're here? You thought I'd know why?"

I nodded again, waiting for her to put together all the pieces. I should've known my mother wouldn't have surrounded herself with anyone who wasn't clever enough to keep up.

"It's him, isn't it? It's your—it's Moriarty." Again the disgust in her voice, like she was incapable of saying the name without it.

"What is in the letters?"

"The letters are everything. The letters are your why. But I don't know how he's stopping them from sending. I don't even know how he could know what's in them."

I knew. I didn't want to let the memories back in, but I knew how. "Mom."

Alice stabbed a finger toward the table as she said, "She'd never do that. Ever. She didn't trust anyone."

I closed my eyes and covered them with my palms. I suddenly felt exhausted, like I'd been at this for days and days rather than a few hours. "She was drugged out of her mind in the end." I dropped my hands to the table but kept my eyes shut. Remembering what I most longed to forget. "She'd call for us, but he wouldn't let us in with her unless she was sleeping. He said she was talking madness, and he didn't want us to remember her like that." I spent so much of my focus trying to keep the tears away, I wasn't able to soften the bitterness from my voice when I added, "As if we couldn't hear."

As if she wasn't ours, too.

Alice's hand fell across mine, and I twitched away from her touch again. "Sorry," I mumbled.

"Did he do that, too?" I didn't have to look up at her to see her gesturing vaguely at my face.

I nodded and then shrugged. But Alice reached across to lay her hand over mine once more, her voice soft but urgent. "She didn't want this for you. She would never have left you with him like this if she had a choice. You need to know that."

I shrugged again. Because it wouldn't be for long. I would get the boys and me out somehow. But figuring out how required focusing on my mother right now, on these people my father had murdered, on what I needed to know and scraping away the rest of it. "What is in the letters?"

"Locations. To the stockpiles."

Like a park planter that might have had more hidden than Mom's getaway identity, or a dug-up square just six paces from a clover carving in the tree, which could definitely have once held a box of money. Had they all died next to their locations? Yes. I was almost sure they had.

"Why Regent's Park?" I asked. "They all died in different places in the park."

Alice stared at the table, her eyes glazed in memory as she spoke. "We all kept ten thousand there."

"Pounds?"

She seemed to snap free of her trance. "After our last job we all met there to split the money. It's where we all said good-bye. A sentimental place, I guess. It was also the only place we all knew about, not that it was much money, really."

"Ten thousand pounds?"

She grinned, though it felt like she was studying me again. "Sorte Juntos was your mother's idea. She always was the mastermind, and this was Ems at her most brilliant." Alice smiled in memory. "Damn. The way her mind worked. It was so simple, so perfect. Her greatest con."

"Con? My mother was a con artist married to a copper?"

Alice's smile widened. "Right? Exhibit A of the 'you can't choose who you love' cliché. But Emily Ferris wasn't just a con artist. She was a master thief. The best I'd ever met. And Sorte Juntos made it so all of us could have retired forever."

I winced away from Mum's name, too quickly realizing the last time I'd heard it spoken aloud was at her memorial. I saw it next to my bed every morning, but hearing it said aloud was different. I wondered what that meant, to have your name go unsaid for so long. "Not everyone retired, though."

Alice shook her head. "Every artist has her own muse. Money, even filthy amounts of money, is almost never the cure—not for a true con artist. It's that moment you know you have them, that's what keeps most of us going."

I held back a laugh. "We've never had filthy amounts of money."

"No?" Alice asked, meeting my gaze with a confidence she hadn't shown me all afternoon. "But you've always had enough—all those years living downtown in London, on a cop's salary?"

I'd never thought about the house, or how we'd come to

live there. Never thought about bills and how they got paid—how all of us had gone to private schools.

"That's part of it. You can't go living high and mighty when you pull off a con as big as we did. You have to stash the money and draw on it slowly. 'Live your best life, not the misery of the wealthy.' That's what your mom used to say. She was the preacher, and we were her choir."

"What was the con?"

Alice shook her head like she wasn't going to tell me, then sighed. "We took down four of the largest targets in London—a bank, a jeweler, a museum, and an airport warehouse. We did them all in teams of three, all in one month, and then we were done. Always the same MO, but always different teams of three, so the eyewitness accounts were always different heights and voices and colorings. And best of all? We were all each other's alibi—well, us and the fifty or so your mom invited to the parties she'd throw on the nights of the heists."

"You got away clean?"

"Clean and with twenty-one million pounds."

"Million? That's impossible."

Alice laughed and shook her head. "Nothing's impossible when it comes to your mom, kid. She was—well, the best I'd ever met. Like I said."

"And you never got caught? Never questioned?"

"They didn't know what to look for."

That sparked something in my mind. A memory of reading words on a screen about robberies and a clover. "The library," I said. "I read about your crimes. That was you?"

"God, you're like her. I can see it in your eyes."

"But you haven't said what the letters are."

"We all hid our money in different places, and the deal was that if anything happened to one of us, letters would be sent out to the survivors to let us know where the money was stashed. We all promised to take care of any family and then to resplit whatever was left."

"And that's what's in the letters."

"Coded, of course. Couldn't have any of it getting out by accident. But your dad shouldn't have been able to stop the letters from mailing. It was all automatic." Alice shook her head. "How did I not see this earlier?"

"Didn't you think it was odd that you never got a letter from my mom?"

Alice shook her head. "No, she sent me her letter. It was right when she found out she was sick. I figured she sent them to everyone then, but now I have to wonder." A flash of fear returned to Alice's expression. "I may be the only one who knows where all her money is."

"You're the only one left," I said again. I felt like it was all I could say to her.

She shook her head. "No. It's you and me. You're in it now."

We stared at each other just long enough for me to compose myself, and then I nodded. "You and me. But that means you let me help you, too."

"We help each other," she said. "And that means I come to London."

"That's insanity. You've got to hide."

Alice smiled. "He won't find me, but I'm not leaving you to deal with this alone."

I should've argued with her, but I found I couldn't. It was a kind of relief to have one other person know and offer help. As she made promises to be in London at the end of the next week and started planning how and where we'd meet up in the city, I felt more and more at ease.

Alice grabbed the picture of the church off the table, the one my mom had left for me in her hidey-hole. "But before you go home, we'll set you up for real." She smiled widely. "This is the fun part."

Chapter 18

Sherlock was in a mood when I finally got back to Lewes. He scowled down at the floor tiles of the train station and didn't even bother to look at me when I walked up to him, which suited me fine. I had enough to think over on my own. My bag felt heavy with the money Alice had stuffed into it. Evidently, she and Mum had shared one of their getaway hiding spots in the cemetery near St. John's in Piddinghoe. It was a bigger hiding spot than the one in Regent's Park and held quite a bit more cash.

"In case you need to get out of that house before I can get to the city," she'd said when I'd protested carrying a brick of money in my handbag on the train. "Southern Rail's got a first-class compartment. Now you can afford it."

Having Alice's help opened up more contingencies than I knew how to plan for, but still a plan started to form. I took advantage of the quiet, but quick, ride to Brighton, where we had to change trains. Sherlock grabbed my hand and wouldn't let go until we were inside the first-class compartment to

London. And when he did let go, he practically flung himself into the seats on one side of the table.

"How was your herb walk?" I asked, sliding into the aisle seat on the other side.

He barely shrugged and turned to stare out the window.

"You're quiet. Did something happen?" He didn't answer, so I tried again. "What are you thinking about?" Again, no answer. I slid over into the window seat to place myself in his direct line of sight, but he looked away as soon as I did, then stood and walked to the other side of the compartment, his back to me.

"What's wrong with you?"

His voice was soft but strained when he answered. "There is nothing wrong with me."

I stared at his back for as long as it took me to decide it wasn't worth indulging this new mood. "Fine. You want to pretend you're the only one in here? You don't have to pretend." I started to gather my things, but I didn't even stand before he relented and spoke.

"I know."

I'd lost patience with his cryptic nonsense, and my tone portrayed that perfectly. "What do you know?"

He turned to stare straight into my eyes. His were blazing. He'd never looked at me like that before. "I know."

"What do you know?" I repeated.

"I know!" he shouted, stomping over to his bag and tearing a piece of paper out, slapping it on the table in front of me. It looked like the killer's page from his wall map. The giant question mark stared out at me, with "Police" scribbled next to it in green marker. "I know. I KNOW!" He shook the page at me, then slammed it back onto the table. "And I know that you know it too."

My heart lurched so hard, I lost my breath a moment. "What do I know?"

"That a policeman was killing people. That he was altering the reports, like that coroner's report with a sentence that left off and was clearly tampered with. I knew it was police, and I knew you were acting weird. I just didn't know it was for one and the same reason until you brought me here."

He flipped the page over. The other side was the flyer for his nature walk, but at the bottom, where he was pointing, was the name of the shop: White's Herbalist, with an address in Lewes. White's Herbalist in Lewes. Reading those words brought the entire text back to me, the obituary of Todd White, the Striped Man from the picture of my mother, whose surviving family ran an herbalist shop. All my secrets undone by a nature walk.

"Neither of us remembered that he was from Lewes," Sherlock said. "I didn't even put it together until after the walk, when they dragged us into the shop to pitch their snake oil. They had a shrine to Mr. White on one of the walls, with a table of candles and baubles and snapshots. His face stirred my memory, but it wasn't until I saw her face that I knew."

"Whose face?" My voice came out as shaken and drained as I felt. And it was a stupid question. I knew who—he'd seen her face on the cover of her memorial program. He'd stared at it for minutes. He knew that I knew as well, which is why he didn't answer.

"All of them in one photo. All dead but one. I'm fairly sure that's who you were going to see today. That's who you couldn't tell me about? Some woman from an old photo you'd tracked down to the middle of Sussex. Did you know them all then? Recognize them from the first?"

His tone held more rough, bitter edges the more questions he asked, and something about that made me angry. Defiant. It was just a stupid game in the park to him, and he had no right to grill me now. "What if I did?"

That gave him pause. "Did you?"

"Does it matter?"

He offered me all the sarcastic bewilderment he could paint across his features. "Yes. Yes, it matters. It all matters."

I looked up at the ceiling and then slid back into my seat. "I didn't know who any of them were, as it happens. I didn't know what it meant or how my mother was involved. I didn't know anything for a long time."

"And you've known who the killer is for how long?"

I crossed my arms. "Ages."

"Tell me how long."

"Never mind."

"TELL ME!"

The train's attendant chose that moment to peek his head into the compartment. "Everything all right in here? Miss?"

I nodded. "We're fine."

"You both get a choice of tea service, fair-trade coffee, or a mineral water."

I took a breath in a vain attempt to calm myself, but still I spoke through my teeth when I said, "Tea, please."

"And for you, sir?"

Sherlock waved off the attendant, which only made me want to smack him.

"He'll have tea as well. Thank you."

The attendant smiled at me weakly, said, "Tea for two, coming right up," and then thankfully left.

I glared at Lock's back. "You're angry with me. You dare to be angry."

"You broke the RULES!" he exploded.

"Rules?" I might have laughed if my voice wasn't already trembling.

"Yes, rules. One rule, actually. We had one rule, that we would tell each other everything, and you broke that rule."

I stood up to face him down. "This isn't a *game*, Sherlock. This is my *life*! It stopped being a game the very moment it became about my family."

"It's not about the game, Mori."

I took a breath and clenched my teeth to keep from screaming at him. "Do tell. What is it all about, Lock?"

"It's about us." He straightened, so that he towered over me, and still he seemed so young to me right then. Just another little kid looking for me to protect him from the truth.

"No. No, it's not. It's about dead people in a park, and my world shattering into a million chunks of iron that are falling down all around me, and I've got no one to help me dig out. That's what it's about, Lock. It's about me fighting off the avalanche all by myself. And I'm so sorry I couldn't fit your rules and your games into the mix this time."

I wasn't sure if he was speechless in exasperation or just had nothing else to say, but he threw himself back into the seats. I felt suddenly exhausted and might have slumped back into mine if he'd kept his mouth shut. But as always, he was incapable.

"You weren't alone. Because I was always there, ready to fight with you. You chose to be alone. You chose it."

I shook my head. Had I actually expected him to understand? "You're right, aren't you? Always right. And here you can be right again. You and your pathetic mind games. How brilliant is the ever-right Sherlock Holmes."

I turned toward the door to stop looking at him, and he reached for my arm. It was such a small space, I couldn't seem to get far enough away to escape his touch. But the very moment his fingers closed around my wrist, I shook him off and turned on him.

"Don't touch me."

He lifted his hands in the air and leaned back, but his expression fell to nothing. He was blank again, even in his voice. "Don't leave."

"What do you want from me? Do you want me to say it aloud? My father is a killer. A serial killer who hunts down my mother's old friends and slaughters them in Regent's Park. Does that make it better for you?" I wiped at my cheeks and slid into my seat again, careful not to allow our knees to touch. I couldn't stand the thought of any part of me touching him right then. "Did you just need to hear me say it?"

He folded his hands in front of him and stared at me, like he was forcing himself not to look away. "No."

"Then what do you want, Lock? If I had said it yesterday? The day before? Would that make it better?"

He didn't answer, and for some reason that made me unreasonably angry. "Do you think I want this? I live in that house. With him and my brothers. And every moment I'm with you is a moment that I'm not there to protect them. I'm the only one they've got left, and there's nothing I can do about that or about him. So what would you have me do about it? Because I'm doing everything I know how to do and there are no answers. So you tell me, Lock. What do you want me to do?"

He was so silent, we could only hear the train noises and the sound of my breathing, which was heavier than it should have been.

The blank of his expression broke right before he spoke, and it pierced through me, so that I had to look away and couldn't in the same moment. "I want you to trust me."

"I wanted to protect you." I responded so quickly, I didn't really have time to think about what I was saying. But it was true. "I had to protect you from this. I had to protect us all as best I could."

"By doing nothing?"

His words slapped out at me and I had to pause until the

sting of it faded. "Not nothing. I did everything I could. I found out who he was killing. I found the woman who was to be his last victim and warned her so that she could hide. And I lived in that house, even when I never wanted to step through the door again, even when every second I had to share the same bloody air as him was torture."

"You could have gone to the police."

"He *is* police!" I covered my eyes and slumped in my seat so that the backs of my hands almost touched the table in front of us. "The police won't help. They never help. And they won't believe it anyway. I've covered his tracks."

"That day you went to the park without me."

I ignored that. I didn't want to think about what an idiot I'd been that day in the park. "I took the sword away from him. He can't use it anymore."

"I saw you leave."

I dropped my hands from my eyes and made myself look at Lock again. I should've been surprised, probably. Mad, maybe. But I was just tired and sad. I was stupid enough to believe I could escape this moment, but it was always coming. "They will never believe he did it without even the weapon he used."

"It doesn't matter. You can tell them what you did. They can find it."

"I already told them I was with him when the last man was killed in the park."

"You gave him an alibi. Why would you do that?"

"I don't know. It wasn't planned—"

"Planned!" Exasperation must have made Sherlock forget

himself, because he lifted his hand to rest it over mine and then stopped himself.

A simple gesture, but it took its toll on me. "I didn't mean to do it, is all."

"Well, it won't matter either. We can still prove it. We'll convince them with logic. I figured it out."

"And then what? If we do manage to convince the cops that all these killings have been done by one of their own—which will never, ever happen—then what?"

"Then he is brought to justice. He is caught."

"Justice." I paused to study his eyes. "Here is your justice. Tomorrow morning every paper will have his face, but tonight it will be on every telly in England. 'Cop Serial Killer! Cop Kills! Tune in for details!' His face will be on every news site and crime blog. And that is only tonight. By tomorrow afternoon my picture and those of my brothers will join his. We will either be the poor helpless victims of his drunken rage, or perhaps they will catch a side-glance in a photo, and we will be the freaks with the DNA of a madman. One of us will surely follow in his footsteps."

Sherlock said nothing, and when I caught him studying my face, I turned to stare out the window at the landscape speeding by.

"We will be separated, forced into the system, and our futures destroyed. That will be your justice. My ruin. And worse, the ruin of three beautiful boys who have lived through his beatings for almost a year now. Instead of help and compassion, they will get the suspicion of a nation, and it will not go away. The story will die off. Our father's face will be forgotten as he rots in prison—if he rots in prison—and still his legacy will follow us forever."

When Lock remained silent, I moved my hand close enough to touch him, though I did not.

"How is it justice for the deeds of one man to destroy those of us left behind? Why should justice punish the innocent? Is that true justice, after all?"

"No," he said simply. "You are right again. Mori."

The way he said my name was odd, but I continued my case, pushing my very real desperation into my pleading. "I have a plan, but I need your silence. At least for a little while. Can you do that for me?"

"What is your plan, Mori?" He said it again, my name. More slowly than was natural. Like he wanted to hold it against his lips.

"I have an aunt—Alice. She's going to come to London, and my brothers and me, we're going to live with her." It sounded like such a fantasy to say it aloud. When I was with Alice, it had all seemed so plausible.

"And your father?"

"Leave him to me. I'll take care of it."

"And he will stop?"

"Of course." I said the words too quickly, but Sherlock's expression didn't shake for even a second. He just stood, gazing at me with his most thoughtful eyes. "With no one else to kill, he will stop. He will leave us alone, and we will stay with Alice. All of us. Together."

Lock slid from his side of the table to mine, just as the train attendant reappeared with our tea. It was oversteeped and lukewarm, like the attendant had served every other person on the train before us. But we drank it all, stared out at the landscape together, holding hands under the table.

We had both been lost in the silence for so long, it surprised me when the attendant came to collect our trash as the train pulled into the station in London. It was just five, which meant we'd get to my house a few minutes after my regular time. It also meant the boys were out of school.

Lock insisted on taking a taxi to Baker Street and kept his arm around me the whole ride home. I stared past his shoulder out the back window, focusing on the raindrops dripping down the glass as my thoughts swirled apart, then spun together into a fine point once again when he leaned in and kissed me. I smiled. "What was that for?"

"You smile in this certain way when I kiss you. I needed to see that smile."

"Just now?"

"Every now. I'm just usually able to control myself better."

I smiled again, and he kissed my forehead and held me close. It all felt so normal, I started to think maybe we'd make it through this. Maybe we'd really keep my father away from us somehow. Maybe we would really all be okay.

I thought that all the way back to Baker Street, until Lock opened the taxi door and I heard the first bars of an eerie, warbling piano play, followed by a bleating trumpet.

Chapter 19

I stared at my front door, frozen, while Sherlock paid the cab. He might have asked me a question, but I couldn't seem to put any thoughts together with that song playing. It was perhaps only a fraction of a second before I started to run for my door, but it felt like twelve eternities of stunned stillness as my mind, enfeebled by my assumptions, tried to make sense of that song being played on that day. Alice was all that was left of his morbid list, and she was safe in Sussex.

I may have used that as a mantra with my every step that brought me closer and closer to the house. I fumbled with my keys, and then the doorknob, as if I hadn't entered this house through this door every day of my life. I threw open the door to stillness, but I knew someone was there. I could feel it.

Dad wasn't in his room, or the kitchen, which didn't make sense. He should have been home. The song was playing. I ran to the French doors that led to the patio, but he wasn't there, either. That left only the boys.

"Freddie!" I called, and immediately Sean appeared out of the shadows, his lip swollen and bloody. He didn't say anything, just looked at me, his eyes hard and his cheeks streaked with tears that had long since dried.

"Mori?" Michael appeared next, red welts slashing his face. He ran over to me and buried his face in my shoulder, so I couldn't inspect his injuries, and immediately started to shake with silent tears.

By the time Freddie limped from the shadows, I was ready to fall to pieces. His right eye was swollen shut, and his forehead had a gash that was still slowly trickling blood into his eyebrow and down his cheek. He was holding his ribs with an arm that looked battered, and his jeans were ripped and stained. "I tried to stop it, like you always do," he said.

That was my job on "Memories of You" nights. And I hadn't been here. I hadn't stopped our father, despite all my plans.

I shook my head and pulled Freddie closer, reached for Seanie as well. "Never mind that. I need you three to go pack a bag. Pack like you won't be coming back for a while. All your favorite things. Seanie, you'll help Freddie?"

"Where are we going?" Michael asked, his words muffled by my shirt.

"To my house," Lock said from the doorway. I watched his eyes take in every detail of the boys and then I turned away, ashamed. I didn't want him to see them this way. To know how I'd failed.

"To a hotel," I said, trying to force myself to smile when I said it, like it would be the most fun they ever had. "We'll stay at a hotel and I'll take care of things."

"Which one?" Sean asked, as if he wouldn't come along should my choice be inadequate.

I smiled and shooed at him with my hand. "Off you go, Seanie. And no packing your whole life. One bag, I mean it!"

Sean and Fred trudged up the stairs, but Michael wouldn't be moved. I nudged him back from me just enough to see his face. He was crying still and it looked like he would have a black eye.

"Tell me," I said, quietly.

"The s-song," he said, a tear dripping down his cheek. "It was playing when we came home from school."

I'd thought I'd had it all figured out, Dad's ritual, his targets, his methods. My ignorance caused the welts on Michael's face.

"Freddie really did try."

I wanted to sink into the floor, but I managed a nod, managed to keep my own tears from showing. "I know it. I should've been here."

"He stopped when Sadie came."

A flare of panic shot off inside, but I tried to keep it out of my voice. "What happened? When Sadie got here?"

"She brought us a peach pie! Can we take it with us to the hotel?"

"Yes, of course, but I really do need to know what happened."

"She pushed her way into the house and Freddie hid Sean while Dad was distracted. Then she started talking really low to Dad."

"Did you hear what she said?"

"Something about constables she met at the park. Dad did that thing where he hunches over when he's mad and said they should just go and find those constables right now. Sadie looked at me and Fred and then said they should."

"She went to the park with him?" My voice betrayed me, and Michael's eyes went wide. "I have to know everything, Michael. This is so, so important."

"D-dad got mad again when he couldn't find his sweater in his room. He yelled, 'Where is it?' and then it sounded like he slammed his closet door. Sadie smiled at us and said that you'd be home right quick, which doesn't really make sense. Does she always talk like that?"

"And then?" I prodded.

"Then they left to go find the constables at the park."

I could barely take in my next breath, but I forced a grin and smoothed Michael's hair. "Go pack, Michael. Quick as you can."

The very minute he turned toward the stairs, I turned to Sherlock. "Keep them safe. Get them out of here and—"

"Where are you going?"

"He took her to the park." I grabbed Lock's arms and stared up into his eyes. "His closet is where he kept the sword," I whispered. "He couldn't find it, but he took her—"

"Go," he said before I finished, but he didn't let go of me right away. "Be careful. I'll be right behind you."

His phone was out and to his ear the second he let go of me, and I heard him say his brother's name as I left, running down our steps, running down the street, weaving through pedestrians like I was a crazy person. I was crazy. There was no way one person running randomly through the acres and acres of Regent's Park would find two other people if they didn't want to be found. And it wasn't as though he would kill her out in the open where anyone running up could see.

Had I the time to indulge it, that thought alone might have tripped me up, halted my breathing. Had I the time to indulge it, I might have fallen to pieces on the bridge, or when I ran into the trees near the college and there was no one there save me and the birds. I went to the most recent crime scene, and there was no one. The tape had been removed and the grass mowed. I went to the place Mr. Patel had died, by the zoo, to the fountain planter, to every place I knew he'd killed before, and when I couldn't run any more and my lungs screamed for air, I collapsed against the bandstand. Of course my addled mind had taken me there last.

The park was shadowed, stepping into the sheer cloak of dusk, that time of the evening when everything seems so clear, but the details are cloudy. I almost gave in, then, to the screaming frustration inside me, to the panic, to the knowledge that he could have killed her fourteen times over already. Instead, I stood and forced my rubbery legs to take me to the shore. I wasn't sure what I was expecting to find there—some sign that his sword really was still in the depths of the lake. My own footprints to prove that I'd actually thrown it in, that the morning hadn't been a dream.

Instead, I found a shoe. A uniform shoe. A girl's uniform shoe with a ragged scuff down the outer side and mud all around the toe. I stared at it for what felt like an unreasonable amount of time but was possibly only a second. And in that second I ran the probabilities. Population of London secondary schools was roughly 625,000 students, 141,000 in private schools requiring uniforms, statistically 51 percent female, leaving only a one in 71,910 chance that the shoe belonged to Sadie Mae Jackson.

But it did. Of course it did. As did the foot inside and the stocking-covered leg that protruded at an unnatural angle.

The next seconds were silence. A buzzing silence that stripped out the typical chorus of birds and insects that followed us all through the park, stripped out the sound of the rain, even the sound of my own breathing. I only knew I took breaths by watching the rise and fall of my chest. I finally forced myself to look up at Sadie, who didn't move at all.

She was my friend, and I'd lured her right into the arms of a killer—a monster who'd left her slumped against a willow tree by the lake, hidden in the branches just feet from where I'd disposed of his weapon of choice. I thought I was hobbling him, removing one piece of his ritual. I thought he had a list and that only those on it were in danger. I'd thought so many wrong things. Turns out he hadn't needed a sword to kill Sadie Mae, only his hand wrapped round her neck. His fingers left pink-striped impressions there. He hadn't even bothered to close her eyes. And I found I couldn't get close enough to reach them.

Someone tried to break through the silence, even taking my hand in his and pulling me into his arms, so that I couldn't see her anymore, forcing me to hear the pounding beat of his own heart. I wrenched myself free of him, but he'd broken the spell and every sound in the entire city came rushing back, including the wasplike buzz of his voice that seemed to come at me from everywhere.

"Stop, Mori. Stop and think. We call this in now."

I held my hand up in front of Lock's face but didn't touch him.

"Mori." He tried to hold me again, but I stumbled away before he could. "We can't just leave her here."

I stared at Sadie Mae again, but she still wouldn't move. "Stay with her?"

"And you?" Lock's look was blank again, but his voice betrayed that expression. He was afraid.

I shook my head. I knew I should stay. Do something to cover for that man. Take away the fingerprints that were probably waiting to be discovered on her skin. Run home to practice lies with the boys until they were ready to swear Sadie Mae had only dropped off the pie, that she hadn't even come inside the house. Covering meant we wouldn't be on the news. We wouldn't be separated. We would be free from the consequences of having a killer for a dad.

Only he would be free as well. And he would still be breathing. I couldn't have that.

I didn't know when exactly I'd decided that my father had to die. But it had been well before that evening in the park. Perhaps I knew it from that first night when Mallory and Day left us in the house with the monster who'd once been my father. Perhaps just two nights before, when I met his eyes across the shadowed hallway. I was taller than him, standing up on the stairs, looking down. And I already knew. It was just this truth that had spun through my unwitting consciousness for hours or days or weeks, until I accepted it fully as the only way.

Maybe that's how one becomes a killer. Not with decision, but with acceptance.

Truly, it was the only way any of this could end. With one of us dead. Once I knew that, it was easy to decide it should be him. It wasn't even a choice, really. More that it fell to me to accept the reality and to act.

But I hadn't accepted that reality in full, not until I stood with rain-sopped clothes that stuck to my body in odd ways, with my hair in perfect curls that only ever appeared when it was wet, with my best friend lying among the roots of a giant willow tree, still refusing to move. I stared down Sherlock with eyes most likely streaked with mascara and tried not to flinch when the first tendrils of rage started their heated path up my spine.

"Stay with her." My voice was a still pool that somehow managed to survive the escalating violent tremors inside me. I didn't wait for his response, didn't stop when he called after me. The silence had returned, as though the heat had seared away all sound. I was surprised I didn't leave a wake of ash behind me as I wove through throngs of people on the streets, clutching umbrellas while typing or talking into their mobiles. I didn't even remember how I got to our front door, but I remembered the noise it made when I threw it open.

This time the house really was empty. And something about that broke my silence again, just in time for the muffled clicks and clacks of the restarting turntable. Maybe it wasn't the song that set me off. Perhaps the heat had to dissipate somehow. But my first victim was that bloody record. I thrilled at the scratch of the needle across its delicate surface, then again when it shattered against the wall. I gripped the largest shard with a torn up T-shirt that was wadded up on the floor and used it to rip a large tear in the sensible brown duvet Dad had chosen to replace the tulips of Mom's bedding. I ripped open his pillow, until the ugly mess of brown and white feathers spilled across the floor. But that wasn't enough. I smashed everything I could find that was his, emptied his dresser drawers, and scattered and ripped his papers.

I'd managed to rip and shred half his clothes from the closet when I saw the box that held my mother's things. I tried to press on and flung a stack of his sweaters onto the floor behind me, but the whirlwind inside had slowed to almost nothing. I wiped a tiny feather from my sweaty, flushed cheek and stared at the box long enough for even my breathing to slow.

I took the box. I took it upstairs with me and began to pack some of my things, including those things of my mother's that I'd kept hidden, and the pictures of me and Sadie that I'd left stuck to my mirror, even when things had gone wrong. When I left, I turned off the light and wandered out the front door like I was never going to return. And maybe that's why I felt so light as I crossed the street and walked over to Sherlock's house.

I stopped on Lock's front steps and peered through the quasi dark to stare back at my house for a while. I wanted to see him come home to the mess, to the nothing that would be the rest of his short life. I wanted to see his panic or anger or indifference. It didn't matter which. But soon the exhaustion of the day caught up to me, and the strain of holding my bags and managing the heft of the box sent me inside. Still, I watched my porch until the very last moment before Lock's door opened. I wasn't quite done with that place, I realized. But I wouldn't return until I had a fully formed plan to end things for good.

He would pay for all of it.

Chapter 20

I'd always been bad at the next part—the waiting. Still, sitting in Sherlock's window and looking down the street toward mine, I felt the power that comes with patience. My rage roiled within me, strengthening, sharpening, controlled. I could control my breathing, my expression, and even the curve of my shoulders, but I couldn't seem to control how and when the image of a slumped-over Sadie Mae hijacked my thoughts. And I couldn't afford to walk the path that kind of thinking would lead me down.

So, instead, I thought of How.

How he would die.

Poison would be something—to surprise him after he'd ingested it and watch him slowly fade, so that my face hating him was the last that he'd see of this world. But it seemed too easy to me. Too gentle a death. A courtesy he'd never offered any of those he'd killed. It also left too many open questions.

And this had to be perfect—no holes, no clues, no questions.

"Can you see your house from here?" Somehow Mycroft had silently appeared. Again.

I couldn't be bothered to look at him, or answer.

He took a noisy, sloshy bite of an apple, and I pressed my head against the window to get away from him. "Why, yes, your brothers are safe and well cared for. You're very welcome."

"Thanks," I murmured. I should've been with them, after all that had happened—but I never could stay for long. I couldn't stand it, the aftermath, with Michael's crying and Freddie's recounting the fight, play by play. Worse, though, was the way Sean would pretend he didn't need to cry or relive what had happened. A nine-year-old shouldn't have a look that hard. He looked most like Dad on nights like these.

I felt a soft brush against my cheek and looked up into Mycroft's droopy eyes. They were crystal blue—much lighter than his brother's—and were focused on the small drop of water on his forefinger. He rubbed his thumb over it, and I held my hands in my lap to keep from wiping at the cool trail the tear had made down my cheek.

"I take it you have no plans to take them back to that house."

Our eyes met for the first time, and Mycroft's widened a bit. "I see."

I doubted he did. No one would believe the level of violence tripping through my thoughts just then. The crease in his brow relaxed as I focused on softening my expression.

"He will never again lay a finger on those boys," I promised, and just saying the words dropped a pebble in the still pool of heat that lay dormant at my core. I squeezed a fist, digging nails into my palm to keep my composure.

Mycroft paused to study my face and then looked back down at his hand. "I think perhaps I should be afraid of what you just said, but I believe you." He backed up a few steps. "And that's enough for me. For now."

He paused again at the doorway. "One more thing."

"Do go away," I said.

"Yes, do," Lock said from the hallway.

Mycroft scowled a bit but covered his irritation with a flourish of his arm, directing his brother into the room. "I was just going to offer to come and get you, dearest of all my brothers."

Lock sighed wearily and brought me a mug of tea. I thought for sure Mycroft would say his one last thing, but when I looked back toward him, the door was shut and he was gone. Lock sat on the corner of his bed, staring at me. I'd had just about enough scrutiny for one night. I sipped my tea and then set it aside.

"How's your mother?" I asked, but he wouldn't be so easily distracted.

"Where did you go?"

"Is she feeling better at all?"

Sherlock pursed his lips and crossed his arms. I turned to stare back out the window.

"Where is she?" I felt a pressure in my chest even referring to Sadie, and I had to clench my teeth to force it to pass. "What did you do about her?"

"I called the police anonymously and stood guard at the bandstand until they came for her, then acted the perfect shocked bystander when they asked what I'd seen."

I made some kind of noise not even I could recognize, but when Sherlock stood and took a step toward me, I curled further into myself and strained to keep my eyes on what little I could see of my house from his window. "What ridiculous theories did they come up with this time?"

"Not a one. They were at their very best."

"Really?"

Sherlock nodded. "Yes, in that they didn't even open their mouths."

He moved closer, and I thought he might sit across from me on the window seat, but instead he grabbed his violin and started to play. I didn't know the song. The melody was simple and repetitive, but haunting. Like a lullaby, maybe, if it weren't played so plaintively. Something that might, on any other night, have soothed us both. But that night, the pleading of his violin became the sound track of my plan. From the first note, it seemed, I knew exactly what I would do to take my father's life. I even knew how I would get away with it. It was perfect. Seamless.

We sat silently after the final note of the song was played, Lock, with his violin still resting beneath his chin, and I, still leaning against the window, trying to see my house from his.

"You're not going back," he said, as if he'd suddenly decided and I was to abide his will.

I caught myself before I grunted out more than half a laugh. "I have to stop him."

"We call the police."

I shook my head.

He said, "They will believe us now. If nothing else, the boys are our evidence."

"They are my brothers, not the boys, and certainly not your evidence." I stared down at my fists and watched my knuckles turn white. "We'll not parade their humiliations in front of uncaring strangers while you try to make your case. You don't know the police like I do. They've seen it all before, on those boys. They've looked into their eyes, seen the marks on their faces and bruises on their bodies. And they walked away and left us with that . . ."

Lock started to reach for me, but his hand still held the bow.

"They won't help. It's left to me."

He walked over and placed his bow across a small music stand in the corner. "And if you can't?"

"I can. Just trust me. I'll stop him, and this will all be over."

If only he'd left it there, I might have spoken only the truth that night. But my Sherlock was a lifter of stones. He couldn't resist peering beneath them, and so he asked, "How?"

"Money." It was a lie, but it was a beautiful lie. Even I, as resolved as I'd become to take the bastard's life, believed it could work. "It's all he cares about. And it turns out I've got loads. But he won't see a cent of it if he kills one more person. I'll send him away with money and Alice will come—"

"—to care for you and the boys," he said, stepping from the corner until he was right in front of me.

"Yes. She'll come to care for us after he's gone—"

"—and we'll all be here, together." Sherlock was perfectly still, except for the fingers of his left hand, which seemed to tick with the forms of chords against the strings of his violin. He was thinking. He was following the contingencies, making sure my solution had a chance at working. But his expression made him seem less than assured.

"It's the only way." I pushed as much sincerity into the words as I could, but I didn't meet his eyes, because I knew there was another way—the one way to forever remove the stain of my father's existence from our lives, from the world.

I stood, forcing myself away from the window, and suddenly Lock's room felt too small. We were too close. And every time I looked up at him, he would stare into my eyes, searching for something I could never let him find, forcing me to turn away. I needed to distract him.

"What did you play just now?" I walked to his bed, kicked off my shoes, and shrugged my jacket off my shoulders to pool in my hands.

He set down his violin and followed me, his fingers drifting up the bared skin of my arms to trace the straps of my top. "Offenbach."

"Is it a lullaby?"

He kissed my shoulder and turned me toward him. I couldn't stand his eyes just then, so I focused on his lips. "It's a barcarolle, a boat song, like the gondoliers sing in Venice."

"I've never been to Venice." *Sadie always did want to go to Italy.* I closed my eyes tight against the thought, leaned into Lock's arms.

He pressed his lips to my forehead, and I held my breath as his lips brushed down my temple to press against the skin of my cheek. He whispered, "Me neither," into my ear, then kissed his way up my jawline so that his lips found mine open and waiting. I needed this, needed him, but he wasn't close enough, not even when I pulled him down on top of me. His kisses were too gentle, his hands too reverent.

I wrapped myself around him, kissing every part of him that I could reach and pulling at his clothes and hair until we were tangled in his bedding, breathing hard, clinging to each other, almost like he was as desperate to keep me there as I was to stay. And it hurt, the wanting, because I knew I had to leave, and I knew he might not want me back after.

Maybe it was that thought that set off the others, but it was as though someone had overturned a basin in my mind and all I could see was Sadie in every memory I had of her, all spliced together with the way I'd seen her last, slumped in the dirt. Dead, because she knew me. I clenched my teeth and squeezed my eyes shut, but I'd already let it go too far. It was true, though. She was only doing what I'd asked. The more I tried to stop the path of my thoughts, the more out of control I felt, until I fisted Lock's T-shirt and buried my face in his chest and fell apart in a way I couldn't have done before then.

Lock didn't speak, he just held me as I shook and gasped and whispered that I'd sent her to her death, how stupid I'd been to bring her into that house, how she'd died for being my friend. He kissed my forehead and temples as I confessed and, when I calmed some, pulled his shirt off to dry my face.

And, just when I felt the sadness shift to anger, just before I could promise aloud that my father would pay for taking her from me, Lock's fingertips brushed against my lips, hushing the words back within.

His expression was almost relieved, but he was looking at me in this new way—perhaps like I was new, like he didn't recognize me for just a moment. But then he kissed me and I kissed him, and I could almost believe that everything was back to normal. Only, I couldn't seem to lose myself to the moment. There was too much to hold inside. Too much I couldn't let him see.

Lock was different too. He moved slowly, lingered in his touches and kisses, stopped to stare at me, like he was trying to take in every detail. I couldn't stand the way he stared. There was too much in his eyes. I turned in his arms, pulling them around me so that he surrounded me like a blanket, and I could feel his warm breath filtering through my hair to my neck.

"Don't leave," he whispered when his breathing started to get deeper, more regular.

His words tore at me, so that I had to compose myself to answer him.

"Just this once more," I said. And then I repeated my ridiculous promise, because I knew he needed me to. "I'll always come back."

His arms tightened around me as he drifted off, only to droop when he was finally asleep.

Not long after that, I stood by the bed and watched him

with only the dim light from the street lamps to illuminate the room. He slept peacefully, even after all that had happened that day. I wanted nothing more than to crawl back into bed beside him and sleep myself. But sleep would have to wait. Just a little while longer.

Chapter 21

I sat in the dark for almost an hour before my father got home, running the plan through my mind over and over until I could perfectly trace the path of it, account for every contingency, answer for every variation. I sat at the kitchen table, as though I were waiting for him to start eating dinner. Maybe I was. I had two glasses and a half-drunk bottle of whiskey set out in front of me—his dinner of choice—and when I heard the stumbling stomp of his shoes on the front steps, I poured myself a glass and watched the swirling liquid settle into a glassy smooth pond of amber.

My father flicked on the kitchen light and stopped when he saw me. He gave me a hard look through narrowed eyes. I wanted to lift the glass and take a sip, but I hadn't been prepared for how my body would react to seeing him. I felt practically every muscle contract, my hands in fists, my jaw set. The faces of his victims played through my mind like a mantra, pausing on Sadie's lifeless face every time, just long enough for me to grip the seat of the chair I sat in and keep from launching myself at him.

"Boys upstairs?" He didn't slur as much as I thought he would after a night at the pub.

"No." I forced myself to take a drink and was surprised at how sweet the liquid tasted, despite the burn of it.

"What are you playing at? Put that away."

I met his eyes over the rim of the glass and took another deliberate sip. Some kind of expression flashed across his features, but I didn't catch it before they settled into his familiar scowl.

He purposely slowed his words. "Where are your brothers?"

I grinned and stared into his eyes, unflinching. "I'm here to buy them from you."

He took three strides and was only a step away from me when he slammed his fist down on the table. The empty glass clinked against the bottle, and with a slightly shaky hand I managed to slosh some whiskey into the tumbler for him.

"Drink?" I asked, and even in that one word, I could hear my control slipping. I didn't want him to be this close to me.

He spit words at me through clenched teeth. "You will bring them home now!"

"Or?" I took another sip, but this one tasted bitter. "Will you call the police? Beat their location out of me?" I pushed his tumbler toward him and sat back in my chair, tried to calm the snarl in my voice. "Will you kill me? Like you did the others?"

Did his eyes go wide? Or was that just what I expected to see? I studied his face as his expression barely flickered from possible surprise to definite scorn.

"You know nothing." He turned his back on me, and it was all I could do not to draw the knife I'd been sitting on and sink it into his back. I could picture me doing it, every step, even the feel of the blade sliding through his flesh, and the relief of knowing he was erased from the planet.

But that wouldn't do. That wasn't the plan. I had to stick to the plan. I cleared my throat and dug my fingernails into the wooden tabletop.

"I know everything. But more importantly, I know that you are done."

"Done?" He laughed and turned slowly back to me. My right hand fell to grip the hilt of the knife. "Who's gonna stop me? Some pathetic little girl playing tough?"

"So, you admit that you have been killing people."

His eyes narrowed again, and he started looking around us. "You playing spy, little girl?" With a speed I didn't know he had, my father's sweaty face was mere inches from mine. I'd barely had time to move my arm up between us. "You recording this conversation?"

I shook my head and smiled as I scraped the edge of the knife up the stubble of his neck. His eyes were definitely wider then, and his surprise turned to fear when he straightened and I matched his movements exactly, keeping the knife to his neck. When his back was to the wall, I let the edge of the blade slide into his neck just slightly, barely a cut and still blood filled the slice. He flinched and his head banged against the wallpaper. It was like a shot of adrenaline through me; I suddenly had a hard time standing still, and my breathing quickened.

"I thought about recording this, but then I'd have to play a part." I slid my knife around to rest against his pulse point. "And I'm done playing parts around a piece of rubbish like you." Again I sliced just deep enough to break his skin and he hissed. "Besides, I don't need your murderous confession for this to end my way. I just need you gone."

Dad thrust his chin forward and glared down at me. "Gone where?"

I pushed out a laugh, but it didn't sound like me. The sound was cold, bitter. "I suppose I could pay you to run, but I'm not sure you deserve that." I leaned into him, pressing the flat of the blade against his skin so his tiny slices dripped blood down his neck. The sight of his blood flowing was another shot—this one burned through me, releasing all my rage. I clenched my teeth. "I am so done giving you chances."

I forced myself to step back from him, to stab the knife into the table as hard as I could, to focus on the plan and not on the way it would feel to slice deeper, to watch his life drain from his face, to let my fingers run through the warm blood as it pulsed from his neck. It might have been the hardest thing I'd ever done in my life to step back, especially knowing what came next.

The back of his hand crashed into the side of my face, jerking my whole body to the side. "YOU STUPID BITCH!" he roared, backhanding me again just as soon as I'd righted myself. I felt blood fill my mouth, and when he grabbed my hair and forced my face up close to his, I spit it at him.

He stumbled back to wipe it from his eyes but never let

go of my hair. "You'll pay for that," he growled into my ear, before throwing me down to the ground. It was almost too easy. He was so completely predictable. I scrambled to my hands and knees and back-kicked at his knee as hard as I could, which sent him to the floor and allowed me to run into the hall.

I pulled all the coats down from the rack by the door and flipped open the bolt and latch. By the time he made it out after me, I was scratching my nails down through the paint of the door, making sure there were chips under my nails. He might have put together what I was doing if he weren't drunk and blind with his rage. Instead, he slapped me away from the door and threw me on the stairs. I spit again, this time toward the carpet.

He was limping as he came toward me, giving me just enough time to brace myself against the step. When he was in range, I kicked out as hard as I could for his same knee, then scrambled to get into his room. Before I made it past, he grabbed my foot and I went down barely an inch short of banging my head against the corner of his bedroom doorway. I kicked at his hand with my other foot until I got free and managed to crawl into his room and shut the door before he could reach me.

I clicked the lock shut and then stood, taking a few seconds to catch my breath and wipe the blood from my mouth. I looked down and smiled at the rip in the knee of my jeans. I pulled at the seam of my shirt as well, until the thread gave and it ripped up the side.

He was already banging his shoulder against the bedroom door when I got the knife I'd hidden under his bed. Two more slams and the weak wood of the door gave way. He smiled when he stormed through it. Smiled. Arrogant prick. He was so sure of his victory, he never saw me in the shadows of the doorway, holding a knife to his throat before he made it another step inside.

There was no fear from him this time, only rage. He actually bared his teeth at me as I walked him back against the wall, both of us trying to catch our breath.

"You played your part perfectly," I hissed at him.

He only grunted, but I pressed the point of the knife into the hollow of his throat, freeing his words. "Now what?"

"Now?" I forced out another bitter laugh. "You haven't figured it out yet? Now you pay for what you've done."

"Killing those slime? I did the city a service getting rid of that crew. You don't know—"

"I know *everything!*" I sank just the tip into his skin and barely stopped myself from pressing it home. But he would know what he'd done. "I know all about the robberies and about the money."

His eyes were wide again, whether from the blood pulsing from his wound or from what I'd said, I couldn't tell.

"You don't get to pretend you're some vigilante copper, ridding the world of some great criminal ring, especially when your *wife* was the *mastermind!*"

"There's things you don't know." His voice pitched higher with his panic, which sent a buzz of adrenaline through my entire body. "Like the money—you know what that money could've done for your mom when she was sick? I begged for the money, so we could try that new treatment, but she wouldn't tell me."

"She knew you couldn't be trusted," I said through my teeth. "And she didn't want that treatment."

"That's a lie! She'd just given up, is all. And I knew, if we just had the one more chance, she could make it. So when she started talking high about the money and the crimes and making with her names, I tracked one of them down, but he wouldn't help! He had her cure in his hands and he wouldn't help!" He snarled out his next words. "And I told him if she died, so would he."

"But not without you getting his money."

Dad lurched at me, and I was barely able to jerk the knife back before he impaled himself. I think he realized what he'd almost done, because he seemed to sober a bit. "And why shouldn't I have it? I didn't know where your mum hid hers, and we couldn't pay for your fancy schools without it."

"So you lured him to the park. Made him show you where he'd hidden the money?"

"They all stashed their last score in that park. Some kind of pact. All that money, buried away, when it could have saved her!"

"So you took it. But that wasn't enough for you. You had to track down the next one and the next one."

"Cons, thieves, criminals—"

"No!" My shout stopped him talking, or maybe it was that

I'd managed to make another small cut in his neck. His collar had gone red with blood. "Sadie Mae Jackson wasn't a criminal. She was just a girl standing up for three innocent boys you'd beaten so badly, their little faces were deformed!" I was gripping the knife so hard, my wrist started to ache. I felt like my whole body was trembling with what was left of my restraint. "Nothing you say changes that. Nothing! You terrorized those boys and me, and then you killed my one real friend. And you don't get to talk your way out of that. You give your life for hers. That is how this ends! And then you burn in the hell of your own putrid nothing of an ever after and that's still not long enough to atone for what you've—"

I hit the floor hard and felt my hand being slammed against the bed frame until the knife fell to the carpet. Before I even knew what was happening, I was completely immobilized and my dad was sitting on my chest and kneeling on my hands, leering down at me, the knife in his hand. I jerked and kicked, but I couldn't get out from under him. I couldn't do anything but wait and watch as he turned the knife on me.

But he didn't point it at me. He rested the edge against his own cheek and then, with a jerk of his arm, left a big gash in his own face. He hissed in pain as he slashed across his chest and then smudged his hand around the hilt and threw the knife across the room. I jerked my head away as drips of his blood sprinkled down on my face. And he was smiling again.

"Two can play this little game of yours, sweetheart." He leaned down so that his face was right above mine, and I turned away so I didn't have to look at him. He pressed his lips to my ear. "And now I'll kill you in self-defense, so I'll no longer have to look at such a disgusting cow wearing her beautiful face."

I thought I'd heard it all from my dad, that nothing he said could ever hurt me again. I was so very wrong. Still, it seemed the very look of me was my only remaining weapon, so I used it. I turned my head to stare him down, but before our eyes could meet, he stuffed a pillow over my face. It was one of the pillows I'd split open in my tantrum, but he managed to pile enough of it over my nose and mouth to stifle any air that might have come through. I couldn't fight. I couldn't move. All I could do was lie there, desperate to take a full, fresh breath, and listen to him explain how everything I'd done would just as easily protect him from being charged with my murder as it would've protected me.

But I knew one thing he didn't. I knew that Sherlock Holmes would avenge me. It wouldn't take my dad from the world, but it would lock him up for the rest of his life.

At least my brothers would be safe.

That was my last thought as I gasped against the pillow uselessly one last time.

Chapter 22

My mind dimmed only briefly before the coughing started. One moment I hadn't been able to get enough real air, and the next there was too much and I was inhaling feathers in an attempt to get more. I was pushed over on my side and someone was lightly smacking at my back.

"That's it, child. Nice and slow. Not too deep yet." He yelled something about a medic, and then my brain seemed to kick back into gear.

"Mallory," I wheezed out.

He attempted a smile, despite the grim expression on his face, and then pushed me back down when I tried to sit up. "Not yet, now. Stay down until the medics come."

I looked around wildly and saw my dad's head pressed into the rug of the hallway as they cuffed his arms behind his back. I saw a shamefaced DS Day glance up at me and then look away as he hauled my dad up with the help of another officer and started for the door, the other officer reciting cautionary rights, as if DS Moriarty wouldn't know them by heart.

"We might not have made it in time, you know, if it weren't for . . ."

"Sherlock." I saw him before Mallory could finish, but it took me another second to put it together. He'd gone to the police. Despite what I'd said, he'd called them. And his expression was a mix of relief and guilt and pain. I'd never seen him emote like that. I idly wondered if anyone ever had.

In the next moment I was barraged by medics and an oxygen mask, which I tried valiantly to wave off. "I don't need it."

My voice must have been too muffled, because the medic closest to me acted like I didn't say anything.

"Just lie down, and we'll get you out of here shortly. Do you have any allergies?"

I shook my head and pulled the mask off my face. "This isn't necess—"

He pushed it back down. "There now, breathe nice and deep for me."

I tried to sit up again, but before I could, I was lifted up and placed on a gurney. They draped me in a blanket and strapped me down before I could think to get up, everything but my arms. And then I was unceremoniously tilted up. Not one of the policemen or techs buzzing around my house would look at me as they wheeled me out of the house and down the front steps. Then, even the second medic toddled off toward one of the police cars, while mine pulled me backward through all the official people standing around.

I got another brief glimpse of Sherlock and tried shouting for him. He might have heard me, because he looked back at the house, obviously thinking I hadn't been brought out yet, and between my infernal mask and the distance, I couldn't correct that thinking. I didn't see him again until I was jerked up into the back of the ambulance. He was talking to a very interested Mallory, staring at the doorway to my house while answering questions, his face once more the blank I knew best.

The medic climbed up and got in my way again, only to start flipping on various machines, pinching my finger with a sensor, and prepping an IV bag.

"Honestly," I said, pulling the mask from my face again. "This is all extremely unnecessary, and"—his hand started coming toward the mask—"I swear to you, if you mash this plastic monster back onto my face one more time, I will shove it down your throat."

He stopped short, then gave in to a half grin. "Well, you'll be feeling better then."

"Quite better. If you could just unstrap me, thank you."

"Sorry, miss. Orders of the inspector. We're to take you to hospital to be looked over." I sighed, which didn't faze him in the least. "Now, if I could just see your arm."

He lifted a needle into the air, and I might have moved onto my next threat, which involved that needle and his arse, but the radio in the front of the truck went off, and he swore under his breath.

"Be right back."

The whole ambulance rocked back and forth as he trudged up to the front, giving me a clear view of the outside once more. I couldn't find Sherlock—couldn't have found anyone, really. The street was a barely controlled chaos, all of it centering around the police car where my dad sat, a medic inside, tending to his superficial wounds while DS Day looked on. Thankfully, no one thought I needed any attention just then.

In fact, no one was looking my way at all. It was my one chance. I freed myself of the gurney buckles, slid the oxygen mask all the way off my head, and with one more look around me, I ran from the ambulance down Baker Street, toward the only place I knew where I could be alone. I just needed to be alone with my thoughts. I needed a new plan. I needed something.

I heard him coming. I probably could have disappeared into the park if I wanted, but I was so tired. I couldn't be bothered to move.

He sat down next to me in the shadow of the bandstand, but not close enough that he was touching me. I wasn't sure if I wanted him to touch me or not. I was very sure I didn't feel like talking. He seemed to know it, though his jerky movements and his trouble sitting still told me he couldn't keep silent for long. He tried lighting a cigarette, but I coughed before he would do more than make the tip glow, and he put it away. Finally, I reached over and laid my hand over his. We both sighed and stilled for a few seconds.

The wind and the trees and the insects made this odd humming, brushing sound that lulled me into a heavenly place where I could let go of every thought—just for a while—live in that blissful emptiness that I almost never could indulge. Even now, it wasn't meant to last for long. The constable in charge of guarding the crime scene at the willow tree cleared his throat. I didn't think he could see me, hidden as I was against the far side of the bandstand, but I could see glimpses of his ginger head and the yellow police tape creating an imperfect circle to surround the place where Sadie had died. The bandstand would never be an escape for me again. My sanctuary had been invaded.

Sherlock slid his fingers between mine and scooted closer, though he wouldn't look at me, not even when he finally spoke.

"I called the police."

My voice was a weak croaky thing from all the coughing. "I noticed."

His face was directed toward me, but his gaze shifted down. He still would not see me. "I tried to let you go, tried to trust in your plan."

He paused, as if I was supposed to respond, but there was nothing to say, really.

"You looked so alone walking down Baker Street, and I didn't want you to be alone with him. Not after what happened last time." Sherlock looked directly into my eyes before speaking again, and there was no disgust there—no pity, only pleading. "When I saw him go into the house, I called the police."

He wanted me to tell him it was okay, that it was for the best. I couldn't say anything. I couldn't look at him.

"I would ask you to forgive me, but I find that I am not sorry." He cleared his throat. "I could not give you up. And I knew, were I not to intervene, tonight would end in one of three ways. Either he would kill you, and . . . I . . ." He cleared his throat again. "Or you would go with him in some deal to leave your brothers behind and out of his reach. But what scared me most of all was that I knew you were clever enough to see what I saw from the moment you showed up on my doorstep today."

He was so quiet, the sounds of the evening insects drowned out even his breathing. He couldn't know. He couldn't. And still, I asked the question that hung in the air above our heads. I didn't even have to think the words, just open my mouth.

"What did you see?"

His eyes found mine again, looking more like mine than they ever had. They were so calculating, I felt a shiver trip down my spine.

"That your father should die."

"Die." I whispered my echo. He knew. Impossibly, he knew. I opened my mouth again. "Why? Why did you stop me? Why bring the police?"

His gaze shifted down again, and I could see him wrestle with his words in the pained expressions that cycled across his face. "If you did this thing. If you . . . You would not be you anymore." He took a breath, but I could not. "And I . . . Mori, I—I cannot give you up. Not now. And I cannot even be sorry about it."

Hot tears trickled unchecked from my eyes. My Lock. The

one man who could not even take credit for saving a life if his motives were known to him to be selfish. I should've thanked him, but even then, watching the pained furrow of his brow, I couldn't help but think through all the ways this night could have ended better if only he hadn't gone to the police. If he'd come to me with what he knew, we could've worked together to end my father. If he had just even come alone, he could have stopped my father from killing me long enough for me to find the knife and finish him. If Sherlock hadn't done the one thing I told him not to do, Dad would be gone, and I would be free. If only I could have stopped him myself.

"He was stronger than I had anticipated," I whispered.

"Don't."

"There was a moment when I knew I could get away, but I also knew—"

"I don't want to know."

"Well, you will know!" I shouted, then glanced over to the crime scene. The ginger head didn't seem to have noticed my outburst. I turned back and stared directly at Sherlock, forcing him to look back at me, but as soon as he did, all my anger fled, leaving only exhaustion behind. "You will know how you ruined—"

"Mori." His fingers traced down the side of my face, along my jaw to my chin. He pulled me close so that he could rest his forehead against mine. "Tell me if you'd like, but it changes nothing."

A sob escaped my lips and I felt one of us tremble. "He hurt me."

His thumb swept across my eyelid and down under my eye, where I knew the skin was probably purple. "The bruises will heal."

"He hurt me." I laughed softly, which only seemed to release more tears. "Even now I hear his voice. I will always hear his voice. . . ."

His hands surrounded my face, and his cheek slid down to rest against mine. "He can't hurt you again."

"It was all so perfect, my plan. And you know what stopped me? My own frailty. I went into that house to prove he couldn't beat me, but he did. Because I was helpless. Weak. And now I'll only ever be that." *Because of you.*

I felt Lock release a breath against my cheek, felt the cool trails of both our tears. He didn't speak for a long time, and when he did, he said, "You are the strongest of all of us."

Flashes went off all around us, even before we stepped out into the open, and I watched as the looming light of a news camera swooped toward me with an almost supernatural speed. Sherlock's arms surrounded me, pulling my face to his chest as the shouting began.

They shouted my name.

They knew my name.

"It's too late," I yelled against Lock's chest. "They know. Everyone knows."

Lock ducked his head against mine and spoke softly, but miraculously I could hear. "They will never know it all. No one will ever know. I will make sure of that."

I felt a stirring in my chest as he held me tighter, pulling us through the fray with a strength and daring I thought he would never show to anyone but me. My most feared predictions played out in front of us, and most of me wanted to push him away, to scream at him for doing this to my brothers and me, for bringing the police and attracting the press. But then we were through the throng, and still he shielded me with his body just long enough to look down and meet my eyes before we walked across the open space between the police tape and my front door.

"Say the word and we'll be eating Mrs. Hudson's sandwiches on our way to Venice." He quirked a smile and stole a quick kiss when I lifted the side of my mouth as well—the closest I could get to any kind of smile on that night.

And there it was, like a light—like the flash as a candlewick takes a flame. I saw the path of my life stretch out before me. Past the humiliation, past the chaos I would endure, past all of that, Sherlock Holmes was still at my side. And there, sheltered in his arms, I made two startling realizations. I knew that I would probably love this boy for the rest of my life. I knew also that I would never, ever forgive him.

Acknowledgments

First, thank you so much to my agent, Laurie McLean, who managed to do in mere days what no one else could do in years. You are the ultimate rock star, and I feel lucky to have you as my partner, advocate, and friend.

Thank you to my super-genius editor, Christian Trimmer, who believed in my fledgling manuscript enough to help me turn it into an actual book. I am so very proud to be a member of #TeamTrimmer. And special thanks to all the brilliant people at Simon & Schuster Books for Young Readers, who championed my book and helped release it into the world.

An extra-special, Red Hots–flavored THANK-YOU to my Writeapalooza Girls: Julie Dillard, Tracy Clark, Temoca Dixon, Dawn Callahan, and Kim Harnes, who have spent countless hours listening to me whine and plot and worry, who have fed me gingerbread, Swedish fish, and Nutella, with plenty of All Business gin on the side, and who never once doubted me. I would be nowhere without you.

Thank you to all the readers who so generously gave their time and insights to this book when it was in its roughest state: Kristen Crowley Held, Chris Woody, Jenny MacKay, Charlene Ellen, Heather Mims, and Lia Keyes. And to the Mentish Group, who let me write with them in haunted hospitals, hotel rooms in Winnemucca, and over Skype when I was too wimpy to face the snow: Craig Lew, Sarah McGuire, Hazel Mitchell, Amy Allgeyer Cook, Jacqueline Garlick, and Nathalie Mvondo (with special guest George the Ghost).

I have also been lucky enough to be surrounded by amazing author mentor/friends to advise and prod me. To Terri Farley, thank you for your A with a hundred pluses and for being the first person to tell me I was a writer. To Susan Palwick, thank you for finding scraps of potential in my writing and going above and beyond to make me pursue it. To Cynthia Cotten, thank you for reading my silly camp journals and helping me to find my voice in YA. To Ellen Hopkins, thank you for advice and wine and friendship and being an amazing example of what it means to be true to yourself and to your art.

And finally, to my family. Thank you just doesn't seem adequate to cover all that you've done for me. But for years of understanding and giving me the time and space to do my work, and for believing in me, even when things got hard and complicated, THANK YOU. To my husband, Tyson, for all your lumberjack calm in the face of my storms. To Gwenyn, for letting me work, even when your more trickstery fairy powers tempted you into my office. To my dad, for countless hours of babysitting and for raising me to believe in the arts. To Norma, my amazing mother-in-law, for listening and tirelessly helping me control the chaos at home. And to my mom: I'm sorry I couldn't make this happen in time for you to hold an actual book in your hands. I love you and miss you every day.